# Shadows Across Time

# Mariah Lynne

Published by
Satin Romance
An Imprint of Melange Books, LLC
White Bear Lake, MN 55110
www.satinromance.com

ISBN: 978-1-68046-166-4

Cover Art by Becca Barnes

*To my husband Jerry who encourages me to write and tell my stories and to my dog Max who reminds me that every heroine needs a loyal pet.*

# Chapter One

The brass bell over the front door to my antique shop, deForet's Finds on Fifth, rang telling me someone had entered the store. A man dressed in a black tunic, tights and hooded cape entered the shop. Odd dress for a Florida tourist. He looked sort of arty. Antique collectors could sometimes be a little eccentric, even downright weird. He wore a gold and bejeweled amulet in the shape of a lion's head on a heavy gold chain. Quite distinctive and probably valuable.

The stranger stared at me and cracked a smile displaying yellow and missing teeth. He continued to approach the counter stopping just short of where I stood. He asked in a combination of French and English if this was deForet's on Fifth owned by a Danielle deForet, a specialist in rare antiques.

I have learned in this business not to judge a book by its cover as the old saying goes.

The man spoke with such a thick French accent I could barely understand him. I consider my French fairly good. After all, I'm of French descent myself, so I could communicate with him in his native tongue.

After a polite greeting, I asked how I could help him. Then, to build rapport, I told him my great-great-great-grandparents emigrated from France and asked him from what part of France he came. Oddly enough, he said, "Chateau de Chenonceau."

My grandmother had told me that in France this castle was the second most popular site for visitors, the Eiffel Tower being first. Its large white structure with imposing blue turrets at its entrance commands a position of honor over The Loire River. I keep the postcard from my aunt on my cash register.

His mention of Chenonceau surprised me. "What a coincidence. My family was also from that region."

I didn't add my grandmother claimed we were direct descendants of a French queen who lived in that very castle. The queen banished my ancestors because someone in my grandmother's family married a commoner. I had listened to grandmother's stories but they seemed so farfetched, I thought she was going senile.

The more we talked the more doubts I had. A strange unease crept over me. His facial skin had a yellow hue and boasted many scars. I found myself staring at him as he spoke to me. He said his name was Alasdair. I thought he meant that as his family name like Smith. After his brief introduction, he repeated the fact that he wanted to be certain I was the Danielle deForet whose ancestors resided in the Loire Valley.

I assured him I was and asked why that mattered. He leaned over and whispered he had an antique 14th century dagger from that region of France. He wanted to deal only with someone knowledgeable about antiques of that era and area.

When I saw him reach inside his cloak, I took a few cautious steps back reaching for the pepper spray in my pocket. I watched him pull out a large object wrapped in brown paper like the kind a butcher might use and breathed a sigh of relief.

He carefully unfolded the package before pulling out the most incredible dagger I've ever seen. It was hard to believe such an intricate antique weapon was on my counter. The dagger was exquisite. I knew I could sell it for tens of thousands of dollars. Large, it had a sterling silver handle shaped like a serpent, its body adorned with diamonds, its eyes with rubies. As I glanced down at the man's wrinkled and deformed hands, I saw he wore a serpent ring that matched the design of the dagger. For a heart-stopping moment, I thought the serpent's red eyes glowed.

This piece was worth a fortune to a collector of that period, a knife collector, or a silver collector. I kept a computerized list of wealthy clients, some of whom would bid for its ownership. Dollar signs dangled in my mind.

He diverted my attention from the dagger by asking me what I knew about the castle. Like a fool, I revealed the story about my heritage and my grandmother's claim to a royal lineage. I told him I put little stock in her claim but since we shared a common connection to the castle, I would take extra good care of his business needs. I added my credentials.

"I'm a graduate of the University of Miami with dual majors of art history and business. My mother started the business and turned it over to me when I graduated. I can show you reviews from many satisfied customers if you like."

He answered in a most insidious tone. "I'm sure you can my beauty. Your blonde hair and mesmerizing green eyes are all I need for credentials. Please give me your estimate of value as well as your charges, but before you do, I would like you to hold it to feel its intricate carvings."

Loud warning bells sounded. I stepped away from the counter to put more distance between us.

"I can't do that. I don't want to incur any liability by handling the dagger without gloves. I'll take a photo of it and do research after the shop closes. By tomorrow afternoon, I'll be able to give you an accurate value. If you're happy with the number, I'll need you to sign some paper work giving me permission to sell it on your behalf. Of course, I'll provide you with a receipt for the dagger. The price could easily exceed $100,000 and I would be happy to sell it on commission."

He appeared interested. "What time may I return for this information?"

Before proceeding to take photos, I told him I should have all the information by one tomorrow afternoon. This strange man seemed happy with my response. When I finished taking photos, he wrapped the dagger and placed it back under his coat.

"Until tomorrow afternoon, my pretty, I can hardly wait."

His familiarity bothered me, but the likely commission on his dagger overcame my scruples. With that, he left.

I continued to go about my normal business trying not to think about the dagger's value. Summer business is slow. That one commission could make this year my most profitable ever.

After the store closed, I researched the dagger's value over dinner. I learned that at auction, it could bring an easy $175,000. The research and photos further revealed its provenance claiming the dagger once belonged to a powerful wizard. Since I don't believe in that sort of thing, I ignored it. However, it might attract some collectors of supposed magical items. I printed out copies of similar items with prices they received at auction. All routine work I do for any appraisal.

The next afternoon, Alasdair returned, looking as weird and menacing as before. "Would you mind locking the door to the shop for security?" he asked.

Since there were some shoppers on the street and knowing the dagger's value, I agreed and put the key in the door. After I did so, he took out the dagger.

I escorted him to the counter to discuss the paperwork. He agreed to a selling price of $175,000 so I reviewed my contract with him. He eagerly signed every page before taking the brown paper package from his inside coat pocket and placing it on my counter. Something about his expressions made me feel uneasy

He kept repeating how beautiful I was. I ignored his comments, having dealt with other lonely old men. My only goal was to get that contract signed. Anyway, the name he penned on the buyer's line was Alasdair of Loire.

Peculiar that he was known by only one name. After he signed, he took a wax seal from his other pocket and asked for a flame. I lit a match and watched him place a seal next to his signature. As he did, he told me he too was of royal lineage and his lineage could be easily traced. After our small talk, I asked if I could examine the dagger again. He agreed.

I reached under the counter for my white cloth gloves but, as I began to put them on, Alasdair asked me to stop.

"My sweet, to truly appreciate the knife's beauty, please hold the handle with one hand on the serpent's head and the other on its body to feel the full effect of the intricate carving."

He stepped behind me as I did so, placing one hand on my shoulder. I tried to ease out from under it but couldn't. My shoulder froze to his touch. Holding onto my shoulder with one hand, he rubbed his amulet with the other and whispered strange words that sounded like an incantation.

Fear gripped me. I couldn't break free.

He waved one hand over my head. I looked up at the ceiling and grew dizzy. The ceiling lights spun and I heard a low guttural sound that turned into sudden crashing thunder.

I watched in complete horror as a black circle of air, a small tornado, seeped under my front door. It scared the bejesus out of me.

The cyclone's force grew stronger and bigger, blowing the front door open and shut before working its way to where we stood. It scooped us up in its black haze. A flock of bats appeared like magic in its coal black mist. They surrounded us as the cyclone blew us high into the atmosphere. We flew as fast as jets.

I looked down as we passed barren landscapes filled with despair and desolation. I was terrified and passed out from fear.

When I returned to consciousness, I was lying on a cold stone floor in a small room filled with glass apothecary bottles. The bottles were filled with colored liquids and powders not to mention small dead frogs, insects, and snakes. When I stood, I felt someone staring at me. I turned only to hear an eerie yet familiar voice. It was that man, the horrid man from my store.

"Welcome to 1559 and Chenonceau Castle. This is the royal home of your ancestors, my dear Danielle."

Alasdair then turned and clapped his hands. "Sir Aidan, please come in and greet our visiting Princess Danielle."

# Chapter Two

The heavy wooden apothecary door squeaked open. I glanced over to see what other horrid human had entered. To my surprise, I saw the handsomest man I had ever seen. He stared at me with clear and engaging steel blue eyes feathered by long blond lashes. His light brown hair, cut in rough layers, touched the bottom of his neck. He looked fit and muscular in the gray knit uniform of her majesty's knights. My heart throbbed. I was terrified beyond belief but still female.

This gorgeous man spoke to the wizard in a soft deep masculine voice. "At your service, Sir Alasdair."

Alasdair waved his hand in acknowledgement. "Good. Please remain by the door until you are asked to escort the lovely princess to her room, but first I'd like to show Princess Danielle a bit of her heritage."

That sinister man in a long black brocade robe approached and took my trembling hand. His touch scorched my skin. I tried to pull away but he stopped me. Alasdair led me to a window overlooking the river. We were far enough away from the knight to be out of his earshot. Alasdair whispered in a gruff tone.

"This magnificent home of your ancestors and is now yours. Danielle, your grandmother told you the truth. You are of royal lineage."

He knew I saw him sign his name on the contract, but for some strange reason he felt it necessary to introduce himself again. Alasdair bowed before speaking in respectful tones as if addressing a royal.

"My lady, my future queen, I am Alasdair of Loire, also known as Alasdair the Magnificent, noted sorcerer and advisor to Her Majesty Queen Katherine of Chenonceau. Her majesty is the reason you are here. She ordered me to summon you so that you may have the privilege of providing her with an incredibly generous and selfless task."

"A task," I asked, puzzled. "For a queen?"

I remained cautious sensing he wanted something important from me. Hard as it was, I looked into his red eyes.

"I can't imagine what task I could perform for a queen. I'm a small shop owner from Naples, Florida. What does she want? Perhaps she wants to acquire one of my valuable antiques. Believe me; I'll be more than happy to give her whatever she wants. Send me home and I'll give her my entire shop."

The wizard looked at me and laughed. "Ah, my lovely, if it was only that simple. She wants something you brought with you, something that is a part of you. Before we discuss the details, I will let you have some much needed rest to recover from your travel. Aidan, special guard to the queen, waits near the door to escort you to your chamber."

Alasdair turned toward the door and called out, "Aidan, please step forward ready for escort."

I watched as this handsome man came forward, bowed, and took my arm.

"Escort this young lady to her room, the queen's special guest room."

Aidan bowed to Alasdair before glancing back in my direction. He had the most fetching smile that showed his dimples. I realized my nightmare with Alasdair would not go away, but seeing Aidan gave me something and someone good to dream about.

Funny, all I could think about was how awful I must look from whatever kind of travel I had just experienced, while Aidan could be a model for expensive men's cologne. Our eyes locked, but he dropped his stare at once. I wondered if I looked that awful, but couldn't ask. His smile left me tongue tied, absolutely speechless.

Alasdair interrupted my wonderful moment with more orders. "Once in your room, Aidan or another guard will be posted outside your door at all times so there will be no thoughts of leaving."

Leaving was all I could think about.

"I'm sure I'll find a way to escape. I can be difficult and will make you so sorry you kidnapped me, you'll release me just to get rid of me."

He then sneered. "Escape? Ha! Where could you go without my help? Tomorrow we will discuss your selfless mission for her majesty. In the interim, I will advise the queen's maids to wash and dress you like the royal lady you are." Alasdair turned away for a few minutes.

I caught Aidan's eyes slowly taking in my body. His eyes darted away when I looked at him. I realized what captured his attention was my manner of dress, which was scandalous for his time. I wore a short blue skirt with a yellow V-neck top.

Alasdair turned back to face us again. He signaled for Aidan to leave.

The knight spoke French making his deep voice sound even sexier. "Is her majesty ready to leave?"

I sighed at the sound of his voice. "Yes. I'm ready."

I continued to hope all this was a dream until I pinched myself. No, not a dream. Aidan was really there, but so was I and so was that wizard.

I took Aidan's arm and allowed him to lead me out the door and down a steep winding staircase that skirted the outside of the tower.

"Please, watch your step, my lady. These steps prove treacherous for many."

I walked one step behind him and am embarrassed to admit I missed a step, falling on purpose so he would have to catch me. I know how immature that sounds, but I wanted to get close to him. When I did, he was quick to grab me and I gladly fell into his muscular arms. His touch was gentle but firm.

A rush of passion flowed through my body as I gazed into those gorgeous eyes. He tried to avoid my stare, probably a royal thing, but relented. When our eyes met again, sparks, or should I say fireworks, flew between us, but again he was quick to turn away.

"Are you all right, my lady? Should we continue or pause a bit?"

"I'm fine. Sorry for the clumsiness."

"No need to apologize. Let me help you rise."

Aidan helped me up asking again if I was able to proceed. After I responded yes, we continued down the staircase until we reached the second floor landing. I looked down at the dark river water passing underneath the ground floor of the castle. Aidan held my arm tight, escorting me through a single door and into the magnificent chateau.

The hallway boasted polished marble floors with blue and yellow painted tiles on the walls. Even with all my misfortune, I felt like the heroine in a romance novel. I didn't have much time to take in my new surroundings as Aidan rushed me down a long corridor. We passed ten doors before he opened one.

"After you, my lady. Please make yourself at home. Feel safe. I will stand guard outside."

"Stand guard? Does that mean that no one gets in or I can't get out?"

Aidan looked down before shooting me another irresistible smile. Those dimples may prove the death of me.

"Both, my lady."

I entered the large bedroom with windows that touched the ceiling and a rose lace canopied bed that only a gazelle could get into without a footstool. The beauty of the antique furniture made my jaw drop. I turned so wanting to explain to Aidan what happened to me, but he had already left, locking the door behind him. There was a slide window on the door. I rushed over and opened it.

"I need help. Please."

Surprised I asked so soon, he responded out of duty. "Yes, my lady?" He unlocked the door and stood at the entry.

I blurted out what I wanted, anxious to see his reaction. "I need to escape. This is a terrible mistake. Alasdair kidnapped me. Please, help me escape."

Aidan looked puzzled as he stared at me trying to figure out if I was serious. My plea did make him enter my room. He was quick to close the door not wanting anyone to overhear my request.

"You are joking, I hope."

"No. I have never been more serious about anything in my life. I was dragged here against my will. Alasdair tricked me to come here from another place and time. How powerful is that man anyway? He is very rude."

"Sorry to hear he was disrespectful. I don't understand why. He is most respectful of her majesty. How could you come back from another time? That's impossible. It must be your exhaustion talking. Please. Relax. Her majesty the queen ordered me to protect you with my life."

The queen? Why would she care what happens to me? I paced around the room looking at the ostentatious surroundings that reminded me of the old castle dollhouse Grandma gave me. I shook my head still hoping to wake myself from a dream.

Aidan walked over to the closet and opened the door. "Maybe you will feel better after you rest. You will find everything you'll need here. I'll call for one of Queen Katherine's maids to assist you." He turned to leave.

I grabbed his arm feeling how muscular he was in the process. "Please stay. I'm frightened," I blurted out. "I don't know why I'm here or what that wizard wants from me."

Aidan stared into my eyes before studying my face. I'm sure he wondered if I was telling him the truth. He listened, patting my arm and trying to console me.

"My queen is magnanimous. I am sure you will be fine. Now I must take your leave. I have my duties." With that, he turned and walked out of the room.

The door closed and locked behind him. I thought I heard him approach the door again. I walked back to the door and opened the small window again. Curious, I pulled the peek through open and peered out. All I could think of were those two steel blue eyes.

"'Oh." I jumped back startled.

No steel blue eyes stared back at me, just frightful black and red ones. Alasdair. What did he want from me now?

When I heard Alasdair speak to Aidan, I had to cover my ears. Just the sound of that wizard's gruff voice made me ill.

"Aidan, unlock this door. Let's see how our newest royal is faring. The queen needs her to be perfect."

The wizard's harsh voice sent shivers up my spine. Trembling with fear, I heard Aidan put the key in the lock and watched as the door opened.

Alasdair swept in wearing his long black robe and heavy amulet. Aidan followed three paces behind. The wizard approached giving me the once over with his eyes.

"I want to make sure my special lady is all right. The queen demands reports of your well-being."

I faced him standing as straight and stoic as I could. "I'm just fine, but I demand to know when I will be going home. I've had enough of your cheap tricks. Amateur magicians are far better at illusion than you."

Alasdair stepped back, unhappy at my response. He appeared as angry as that fire-breathing serpent on his dagger. His eyes glowed red and his breath smoked. I wanted to make him so mad he'd be sick of me and send me home.

"You're brave," Aidan said. "You realize sorcerers with his talents could just as easily make you disappear."

I shuddered, thinking, *a little late now.* "I didn't think of that." Anyway, Alasdair calmed himself down muttering he must remain steady to grant the queen's wishes.

There lies the puzzle. Why on earth would the queen need me to have her wishes granted? I thought he mixed me up with someone of the same name. I Googled myself once before all this happened and found twenty Danielle deForets.

"Are you sure you have the right woman? I'm not magical and can't grant any wishes. If I were, I would have left hours ago. You, mighty Alasdair, have the wrong princess."

Alasdair looked furious, but he responded all the same. I couldn't help but wonder what was in it for him.

"Of course, you are the right princess. Enough of your insolence! Aidan will bring you some food and afterwards call for the queen's maid to bathe and prepare you for tomorrow's meeting with her majesty. Do you understand my orders, Aidan?"

Aidan nodded.

The sorcerer stared into my eyes with that ugly red glare of his before turning and leaving as quickly as he had entered. Aidan followed. It was hard for me to accept that Aidan could play any part in the wizard's scheme. I paced around the room trying not to let my despair get the better of me.

It seemed like hours passed before I heard someone unlock my door again. I peeked through the small peephole to see Aidan carrying a tray with bright purple peonies on it. Just the sight of him cheered me, if only for a short time.

"My lady, I have your supper. The tray is hard to maneuver through the door. May I bring it into your room?"

How could I refuse a kind request from a handsome man?

I lifted the latch and opened the door wide enough for him to carry the tray inside. Aidan entered, walking past the new guard on duty while carrying the large silver tray with covered plates and a lovely Limoges china teapot.

I looked at the teapot. It was exquisite early Limoges soft paste porcelain from St. Cloud, a blue and ivory oriental design. Antiques are in my blood.

I looked at the dinner service, fit for a queen. Aidan took the tray to the large round table by the window and set it down. Moving an upholstered chair next to the table, he bowed.

"Your supper awaits, my lady. You looked so forlorn when I left that I took it upon myself to pick some flowers from the queen's own garden to grace your tray. Please sit and enjoy a hearty meal."

Aidan moved the chair out for me. "If it pleases my lady, sit down."

He held the chair. I sat down and he pushed me nearer the table. He placed the plum linen napkin on my lap and uncovered the various dishes filled with soup, bread, and chicken cooked in a sauce.

"Would my lady like to have me taste the food to make sure it's fit for Your Highness?"

I must be dreaming. My eyes couldn't help but soak in his muscular body as he stood beside me.

"Is tasting a normal custom?"

"No, only for a future queen such as yourself."

"A future queen?" I looked him in the eyes as I spoke, but saw that my stare made him uncomfortable. "Well then, my knight, please taste my supper; but do sit with me as you do."

That suggestion disturbed him even more. "My lady, that is not proper."

I responded with a royal command. "It is if I order you to sit with me."

Aidan looked puzzled. He didn't know how to respond. My royal command worked because he sat down and tasted the food. He tasted a small amount of soup, a small berry, a tiny piece of bread, but took a big forkful of chicken cooked in a wine sauce. It smelled like a dish my grandmother made. He handed me the fork. I took it from him and stabbed a large strawberry slowly moving it to his lips.

He tilted his head back trying to avoid my advances. "My Lady, as I said before, this is quite improper."

"Oh, but this berry looks so delicious. So fresh and juicy. I know you'll like it."

His face broke into a shy smile, making him blush as he opened his mouth to let me feed him. "Please, I must leave before Alasdair returns."

I nodded taken by his kind manner. "Thank you for bringing supper and the lovely flowers."

Aidan stood to leave. "You are welcome, your highness."

As he turned, I surprised him by grabbing his sleeve. "Please stay. I would appreciate the company of someone I do not fear. I command, you stay." I hoped that would work.

"As you wish, but you must explain to Alasdair that you ordered me to stay," he responded before sitting down again.

"I will. Alasdair must have great powers in this castle for everyone to be so afraid of him."

"My lady has no idea how strong."

I was hungry. Odd, my stomach should be too upset to eat after everything I had been through, but the chicken stew was as delicious as my grandmother's. The bread was crusty and the red wine beyond compare. I talked through dinner hoping to build rapport with Aidan.

"Have you been a royal guardsman long?"

"Twelve years, since I was seventeen. Guarding the monarchy is a proud family tradition. At sixteen, I went to war to protect the queen from an enemy invasion and threat to the castle. My reward for loyalty was to remain at the castle afterwards and protect her majesty, Queen Katherine."

I answered in between bites. "Your duty here is far superior than risking your life in battle."

Aidan responded like a true warrior. "I serve my queen wherever she needs me."

I noticed he began to relax a little so I touched his arm. He pulled away, but I reached for his hand and massaged it. This time, he seemed to enjoy it.

"You make my task extremely difficult, your highness. You are so beautiful. I am not supposed to look at you yet I can't do that. I am ashamed to admit how much I admire you. Please forgive me for saying."

"Forgive you? I would hate it if you weren't attracted to me. I'm attracted to you as well."

I moved my chair closer to him. By now, he did not appear surprised by my boldness. I think he was becoming accustomed to me. His eyes filled with intense passion as his gaze took in my body.

Could I be falling in love? I never believed in love at first sight.

I closed mine and leaned in for a kiss. He moved closer to me. His lips almost touched mine when he jerked back and stood.

"My lady, forgive me. I find you most attractive, perhaps too much so. You are the most beautiful woman I have ever seen, but Alasdair would have me killed for saying so. Our conversation was improper and must be kept private."

My body still tingled with anticipation but I pulled back. "You are right. I'm sorry. My behavior was wrong. Please don't hold it against me. I'm afraid I'll never go home again and needed to feel the comfort of a friend."

Aidan's eyes filled with compassion. "I'm sure you will go home. You are the future queen. Alasdair said so. I must take your leave now before I forget myself."

Aidan bowed and left taking my tray with him. At first, I hate to admit, I needed him to serve as a diversion from my worst fears, but as our time together increased that diversion took a firm hold on my heart.

A few minutes later, I heard a gentle knock. A sweet female voice followed.

"My lady, please open the door. It's Jacqueline, her majesty's maid. Don't be frightened. Aidan requested I prepare you for your meeting with the queen tomorrow. May I enter?"

"Yes. Please do. I have just finished my supper."

The door opened and a beautiful young woman dressed in rose-colored layered ruffles and white lace entered.

"I have been assigned to be your royal maid for as long as you reside in the castle. Alasdair ordered me to take the best care of you."

I looked at Jacqueline. She was as beautiful as her name. Young, blonde, and well groomed, she approached and curtseyed.

Because I watch a lot of period movies, I knew to return the curtsy. Jacqueline called out into the hallway for another maid named Cecile, not as well dressed, to bring in the kettles of boiling hot water. Cecile filled my pink marble bathtub with them before adding fresh rose petals and colder water from another bucket.

Jacqueline escorted me into the bathroom and helped me undress. I reluctantly got in the bath, but once in, the fragrant water soothed my aching body and cleansed my fearful mind. After my bath, I was brought a white cotton nightgown with lace ties.

Jacqueline spoke, avoiding any eye contact. "May you rest well tonight, my lady. I'll leave a dressing gown at the foot of your bed and will return after your breakfast to dress you for your meeting with the queen. I have been instructed to make you look your best."

She then said something that struck me odd. "You resemble a portrait of the queen as a young woman." She lowered her voice to a whisper. "Stay alert, your highness. The wizard Alasdair may enter your room at any time without notice. Listen for his heavy footsteps and heed the foul scent of his breath. It smells like burning smoke."

With that, Jacqueline and Cecile curtsied and left. I waited a few minutes before running to the peek-through to see if Aidan stood guard. To my disappointment, a new guard stood there. I didn't want to call attention to my interest in Aidan so I didn't ask when and if he would return.

# Chapter Three

As luck would have it, Aidan returned very early the next morning, at sunrise to be precise. He tapped on my door holding a breakfast tea tray. I put on my dressing gown before opening the door. Aidan entered, closing the door behind him and placing the tray on the table.

I walked over and took his hand. "Thank you, Aidan, for all your kindness. You have no idea how comforting it is to me after all I've been through."

I leaned in and kissed him on the cheek. He shot me a boyish smile before warning me.

"You must be very careful my dear lady. Alasdair has eyes and ears all around this castle. Please sit and enjoy your breakfast. Castle rumor has it they are taking you to meet her majesty the queen this morning."

Lifting the napkin off my food, Aidan tasted a spoonful of oatmeal. I sat down but didn't feel very hungry. I ate a mouthful. The oatmeal was tasteless without any cinnamon or fruit. I pushed my bowl aside.

Aidan pushed it back. "You must eat to keep up your strength. I'm sure you will need it to face whatever Alasdair has in store for you."

Not wanting to appear obstinate before my dream lover, I did as he advised. Besides, I knew if I were to escape, I had to be strong.

Once finished, Aidan took my tray and left. A few moments later, there was another knock on the door.

It was Jacqueline who returned to dress me and fix my hair. She was carrying a two- piece gown of mauve satin with a violet lace overlay and a matching violet lace jacket, which she hung on the closet door. She helped me through the layers of undergarments before assisting me with the gown.

"My lady, you look beautiful. The queen will be pleased. Now let's

16

take care of your unruly hair."

Jacqueline brushed and combed my long hair before braiding it in French braids and placing fresh flowers throughout the braids.

"The pink flowers compliment your blonde hair. Now you look like the crown princess in her majesty's court."

She took a small black velvet bag out of her skirt pocket. My eyes couldn't believe its contents—an intricate pearl, diamond, and tanzanite necklace. Jewelry fit for a queen. Jacqueline had me turn so she could fasten the clasp of the necklace. When she was finished, she walked me to the mirror again.

"You are magnificent, your highness."

She curtseyed as I marveled at my new appearance. I couldn't believe how she transformed me into the princess my childhood self often dreamed of becoming. It didn't take long before the door burst open again. The maid kneeled as an impatient Alasdair stomped inside.

He walked around me, eying every last detail of my appearance.

"You've done a wonderful job, Jacqueline. The queen will be pleased when I tell her how you turned this common wench into a future queen. You are excused and may take your leave."

Jacqueline curtseyed and left. I shuddered at the thought of being alone with that evil man. He came closer. Taking a monocle out of his top pocket, he grabbed my face by the chin and held it up to his spectacles.

"The resemblance is truly remarkable. You could pass for her majesty's double in her younger years. Your grandmother told you the truth. You are of royal blood. My search for Queen Katherine's future relative is now a success.

"I was able to locate you by snatching the thoughts of an old acquaintance, another seer. She projected happy thoughts of you; her mind casting them into the atmosphere easy for a clever sorcerer like me to catch. It was so easy, it seemed like she wanted me to find you, but won't she be upset when she discovers that I did." He rubbed his gnarled hands together in satisfaction.

"Danielle, you are our future queen. I have big plans for you, but I cannot share what they are just yet. You are to come with me to the throne room, but first I must instruct you on royal protocol. You must approach the throne only when asked by her majesty. You must not look her in the eyes. You must curtsy and always call her your highness. I'm sure you're a smart enough young lady to absorb all of that."

Alasdair turned to face the door. "Aidan, are you out there? Prepare to escort us to the throne room."

There was a quick knock. The door opened and Aidan entered. His face was stoic but his eyes couldn't hide his delight at my transformation. His longing stare vanished replaced with one of concern once Alasdair took my arm and placed it in his. We left the room with Aidan leading us through the dark narrow corridors until we reached the throne room. My handsome knight entered first. I trembled at the thought of meeting the queen imagining her to be a female version of Alasdair.

"Your Royal Highness, Queen Katherine, I present the Wizard Alasdair and the Crown Princess Danielle deForet." He clicked his heels together and backed away.

Queen Katherine was quick to respond. "Ah, yes. I have been waiting to meet Danielle. Tell them to enter." Her voice was soft and very feminine.

Aidan turned to face us. "The queen requests your presence in the throne room."

Alasdair jerked my arm and we entered this magnificent room. My eyes absorbed the opulence of the surroundings. Gold gilded furniture, royal blue velvet drapes, French tapestries, and wine colored carpeted stairs leading up to the queen's gold throne. I was in awe of the room's beauty, but not enough to forget I was scared out of my mind. We walked up the runner stopping directly in front of the throne.

Alasdair introduced us. "Your majesty, Queen Katherine, it is my privilege to present your future heir, Princess Danielle deForet."

Future heir? Am I going to be queen? Will she abdicate? Somehow, I didn't think so. Something was up and it didn't bode well for me.

The queen motioned us forward. "Yes, my most trusted wizard. Bring her here to me so that I might inspect her youthful face."

We approached, stopping at the base of the royal stairs. Alasdair kicked my ankle and I curtsied. I stayed down not looking directly at the queen even though I watched her red velvet shoes approach me. I marveled at her small feet as the queen continued to walk around me.

"Amazing. She bears an uncanny resemblance to my younger self. She's quite lovely if I say so myself."

Queen Katherine stopped, ending in front of me. "Young lady, stand

and state your name."

Alasdair gave me a small tug. I rose.

"My name is Danielle. Danielle deForet."

I caught her smile out of the corner of my eyes. She was beautiful for her age. I guessed mid-forties with dark blonde hair, green eyes, and fine features. She could be me in twenty years.

"What an appropriate name. Danielle of the forest. We do have dense forests here. I'm sure one of your clever relatives whom I banished to the woods came up with that name."

She stepped closer and touched my face. I didn't like the idea, but was afraid to move away. Alasdair stood next to me.

"Your skin is impeccable. So even. So smooth. So youthful."

Queen Katherine clapped her hands. "Everyone except the grand wizard and young lady leave the throne room now. I need privacy. Guards stand outside the door."

Ladies-in-waiting wearing gem colored dresses and the extra guards hurried out of the throne room. The queen waited for the room to empty and for the last guard to close the massive doors before speaking again.

"Alasdair, how old is Danielle?"

"I believe from my research she is twenty-eight. Her present age will not change. Once you assimilate her youthful body, you will remain twenty-eight for as long as you wish. Forever, if that pleases your highness."

The queen laughed. "That should give me enough time to enjoy all my young lovers. What will become of Danielle? Will she seek her body back?"

"Let's just say she will no longer exist."

Queen Katherine looked sad. "That's too bad. She seems like a nice young person, but we can't have everything, can we? Tell me, how long will the actual physical transformation take?"

"Depending on my skills, I estimate five hours. We will need total privacy and complete quiet. As you begin to take on her youthful characteristics, she will become weak as parts of her meld into you. When the process is complete, Danielle will be no more and you will have her youth. I shall conjure a spell for anyone who knew her to forget she ever existed. Her own mother will believe she had no children. Her store will vanish in just those few hours as you, my most lovely queen, will start life over again at twenty-eight."

Understandably, the news struck me hard. My knees buckled. Alasdair caught me before I fell. He pulled me to my feet.

Katherine continued. "You have given this much thought. You are sure no one will miss her? Does she have a wizard?"

"No one will miss her. She is alone and married to her work. Not many relatives except the mother I mentioned and a cat. No boyfriends, no lovers. Lucky for us, she is a loner with the proper blood lines."

The queen nodded. "You've found my perfect match. That's why your skills excel those of all the other wizards. Now, let me see her eyes."

I couldn't stop shaking as she grabbed my face again and looked into my eyes.

"Perfect again. Sea green." She clapped, happy at that thought.

"Let's schedule a date for this long awaited transformation right now. I'm tired of being an old woman of forty-four. The cold air makes my knees creak. I need a bounce in my step only the gaze of a young lover can provide. For the moment, my trysts are with older men or young men needing favors from their queen. I miss being free and desirable. I miss all the young knights and royals waiting in line to romance me. Alasdair, please do this as soon as possible."

Alasdair bowed. "Of course, your highness. As stated, there is much preparation involved. I must first gather all the herbs and potions necessary as well as take some body samples from each of you. I will then have to review my book of spells for all the incantations needed for such a difficult transformation. I think one week from today would be the soonest."

The queen nodded. "Than one week from today it is. I can't wait. I shall schedule a ball inviting the most handsome young men in my kingdom for my very first evening of rejuvenation. I shall order the maids to prepare my royal suite that day with flowers, champagne, and strawberries, perfect for entertaining my young suitors. Just like the old days. Oh I am tingling all over at the thought."

Alasdair looked disappointed. "I hoped, your majesty, that after I give you Danielle's youth, I, your humble wizard, will be the first to satisfy your romantic desires."

That thought sickened me. The queen, however, was quick to respond.

"Make this happen and I will give you the most romantic night of your miserable life. You and Danielle may leave now."

Alasdair breathed a deep sigh of relief.

"Thank you, your majesty. You are most kind to reward my humble efforts."

Once in the massive hallway, he looked at me with his glowing red eyes.

"You and I, my lovely flower," he said, rubbing his wrinkled hands together, "will get to know each other much better in a week. I can't wait."

The knight, Aidan, stood near the entrance to the throne room. By the look on his face, I sensed he overheard everything.

Alasdair signaled to him and the two men escorted me back to my room. All the way, my only thoughts were of escape.

Once there, Aidan unlocked the door before taking his position as guard in the hallway. He watched helplessly as the wizard shoved me inside, closing the door behind him. Alasdair walked toward me, eyes burning red as he reached for me. I avoided him as best I could, but the room was only so big. He managed to grab my arm and pull me toward him.

"Remember, you and I will become very close very soon."

With that, he held me and tried to kiss my lips. I turned, but his hot burning breath scorched my neck as if it had been singed by a lit cigarette. Alasdair let me go, shoving me on the floor.

He turned to me before heading out the door. "You are one spirited woman, Danielle. That does not repel me, but makes me desire you all the more. I like my women beautiful, independent, and spirited. We will meet again soon, my pretty, for some strands of hair, some blood, and a few scrapes of your alabaster skin. Don't worry, I won't scrape your face just your arm. Do not try to alter your appearance in any way or I shall have to kill you. Do you understand?"

All I could do was nod. I wanted to scream for help at the top of my lungs, but wouldn't allow myself to do it in front of that horrid man. He turned and left, slamming the door behind him as I gazed around the room desperate to find an escape route.

21

## Chapter Four

I paced back and forth, thinking about escaping. I thought about jumping out one of the windows, but they were made of leaded glass and impossible to open. The queen designed this room to be a prison for her royal guests. No way out, not alone anyway.

My mood darkened. I pounded on the walls looking for any defects or hidden doors. I stopped when I heard a strong knock followed by a warm masculine voice.

"It is Aidan. I have your luncheon tray if it pleases you."

Aidan. Just the sound of his voice elevated my mood. I rushed to the door and opened it. He looked so handsome. My eyes took in his slim body and his rugged biceps with one slow steady glance. I closed the door after he stepped inside.

His first words surprised me. "My lovely lady, I know we have only known each other a short while, but I miss being alone with you. Your meeting with the queen has been of great concern to me."

He put the tray down on the table before turning and looking into my eyes. His glance invited me to come closer, but I didn't need an invitation. Walking over to him, I surprised him by putting my arms around his waist. I pulled him in for a long tender embrace. I held him as tight as I could. His affection helped me forget my dreary fate. This was all happening too fast but I never wanted to let him go. Our lips met for a sweet kiss before he backed away from me.

"My lady—"

I placed my finger over his lips. "Please, Aidan, call me Danielle."

"Danielle, I remained close enough to the throne room entrance to overhear Alasdair tell the queen his plans for you. I can't bear the thought of what that evil man and the queen are plotting to do. I am falling in love with you. I don't want to lose you forever. What are we to do? I have to get you out of here. He can't make you vanish into thin air just like that. It would be torture for me to see the queen look like you, knowing all along that her wicked interior remained the same. Alasdair said the transition is set for next week. That gives us little time to plan."

A plan? Aidan said a plan. I put my arms around him again and hugged him as tight as I could. He returned my embrace.

"Aidan, we have to be careful. Alasdair will kill you if he found out."

Aidan looked deep into my eyes. "You are unlike any woman I have ever met. I loved your strength and beauty the first day I lay eyes on you. Every time we meet, those feelings intensify. I no longer care about my fate—only of being with you."

His gaze said it all. I leaned in and gently kissed him again. This time he was eager to return my advances. Our lips locked in a long passionate kiss. He deepened the kiss before moving his lips down my neck.

Aidan took a sudden step back. "This is quite improper. Forgive me your highness. I must come to my senses. You are of royal blood while I a commoner."

I took his hand and squeezed it. "Aidan, Alasdair kidnapped me. I am as common as you."

He listened, surprised at my comment. "How can that be? He says you are a future queen."

I held his other hand wrapping his arm around my waist. "Trust me. I am telling you the truth. Please, I need to feel your strong arms around me for comfort."

When he held me again, I melted in his arms. His muscular hands were gentle as they caressed my body. He kissed me, devouring my lips in his. For some reason, I felt the urge to show him my true feelings. I was scared not as I was of Alasdair, but afraid of being abandoned by love again. I haven't been able to open my heart completely to a man since I lost Josh. Aidan's feelings were as shaky as mine because he pushed me away again even though his eyes were filled with desire.

"I apologize for my boldness, Danielle. I mean no disrespect. I loved you the first day in Alasdair's workshop. I admired how brave you were to stand up to that powerful wizard. You looked beautiful. Your golden hair glistened in the filtered sunlight coming through the small window. I knew my feelings would be considered treasonous, but not knowing how much time we will share together, I want to show you how I feel with every beat of my heart."

His eyes glazed over with passion. I believed that with every beat of mine, he would risk everything to save me. I had fought falling in love for years, fearing I would be left with a broken heart again. However, for some reason I couldn't explain, I wanted to hold him close to me.

Love at first sight? I don't know what happened to me, but my feelings were too strong to ignore. Deciding to give love a chance, I leaned in kissing his nose before moving my kisses down to his lips again.

"Aidan, it's just all this is happening too fast. I think I'm in love with you and desire to show you how much as well."

I pulled Aidan close to me again. I hugged him tight against my body. He trembled. I sensed how nervous he was, knowing we were about to become illicit lovers punishable by death. That made our romance even more exciting. Our lips locked like someone threw away the key. We stood there holding each other as all the cares of our two worlds disappeared.

Aidan took my hand, kissed it, and knelt on the cold stone castle floor. His stare begged my attention. I answered willingly. I knelt down on the floor next to him. We kissed and embraced. At first, our kisses were soft, but it did not take long for our passion to intensify. His kisses grew more passionate. I felt his warm lips move down my neck and onto my shoulder. He stopped for a brief moment, stood, and took his cloak off placing it on the floor. Taking my hand, he helped me lay down on it before he did the same. He unlaced my bodice caressing and kissing my breasts. Passion overcame me.

"Danielle, I want you to know how deep my love is. How much I desire you."

Josh had been gone for three years. I thought about him every day. How could these feelings for Aidan take hold of my heart so quickly? I slithered out of my skirt and petticoats. Aidan helped me stand as we began to undress each other before lying back on the cold stone floor.

The stones' icy surface sizzled from the heat of our naked bodies. Aidan's gentle kisses touched my nose before kissing every inch of my body. I turned eager for him not to miss a spot. He was the most sensual lover I ever had. He moved back up my body delivering wet kisses as he lingered on my breasts. Then Aidan moved on top of me and we made love.

My heart raced. My body tingled with such intensity I couldn't catch my breath. We held each other close before enjoying each other's body a second time.

Our lovemaking ended all too soon. Loud footsteps in the hall approached the door and interrupted our secret pleasures. We knew we risked our lives, but were so absorbed in the passion of the moment we didn't care. Just the thought of impending danger made our lovemaking all the more fervent, all the more passionate.

We were like giddy high school seniors under the bleachers, even though we knew if that was Alasdair, we were both dead. A hard knock followed making Aidan jump up first and struggle to put on his uniform. He helped me stand. I dressed as fast as I could, but those layers of fabric will prove the death of me, literally. Aidan had to assist.

The solid knock sounded one more time. We breathed a sigh of relief. It wasn't Alasdair. He would have walked in unannounced. A male voice soon echoed through the keyhole.

"Aidan, 'tis Samuel. Everything all right in there? The guard shift is about to change. We haven't seen you in the hall for quite some time."

"Yes, I am sorry for the delay, but my lady's closet door was broken. Now that it closes properly, I'll be right out."

Aidan whispered in my ear, "Be patient, my love. I plan to meet with a trusted contact in the village after my guard detail this afternoon. I may have news of an escape plan by late tonight. I will see you as usual in the morning. Remember, I love you."

My body still tingled. "I have fallen in love with you as well. You stole my heart."

With that, he left me to my lunch. I was not very hungry thinking about my impending fate, but I ate some of the stew and crusty bread to keep my strength. A few minutes after I finished, Samuel knocked on my door. I opened it a crack.

"May I remove your tray, my lady?"

"Yes, please come in and take it."

As Samuel removed my tray, I looked out my window to see Aidan riding over the bridge headed to the village.

\* \* \* \*

Aidan had heard gossip about an underground group of villagers who helped political prisoners whose only crimes were disagreeing with the queen or her wizard. This underground group helped many men and women escape the royal dungeon in time to avoid their date with the executioner. They had a contact at the Old Iron Horse Pub. The contact acted as a scout weeding out the truth from the traps.

He had to be shrewd enough to discern if the person seeking help was working undercover for Alasdair and the queen or in desperate need of help. Once affirmed by the scout, that person would learn the secret whereabouts of the resistance leader, a man named Simon the Blacksmith. Simon hid deep in the forest moving whenever the queen's guards came too close. There was a hefty bounty on his head, making him the target of the guards who wanted to find and kill him.

Because the Pub was the favorite watering hole of locals and guards alike, it would not appear unusual for Aidan to go there. He planned to visit the pub that day when he finished his duty.

When Aidan arrived in the village, he hitched his horse to a post outside the Old Iron Horse Pub. He opened the heavy oak door, went inside and perused the customers and staff. Since he recognized no one from the castle, he felt comfortable poking around for information.

He approached the tall wooden bar before sitting down on a stool. Downing a few ales, he asked the bartender if he had seen or heard of a man called Simon the Blacksmith. The bartender didn't respond. Because of his uniform, Aidan suspected he feared a queen's guard. Since he wouldn't respond, Aidan turned and asked the customers seated at the nearby round tables.

"Here, here, I need the skills of a good blacksmith for my steed. I'm told Simon is the best in the land but has moved his shop. Does anyone know where? Anyone seen him lately? I am desperate to have this work done and will pay well."

The men in the room grew quiet. Not one responded. They all turned their backs to him. After a few minutes, conversations resumed. A gruff looking older gentleman dressed in multi-colored rags and using a tall walking stick moved from the back of the room where he sat alone to the stool next to Aidan at the bar. He leaned in stroking his long gray beard.

"Young man," he whispered, "why do you ask about Simon? I see you are in the queen's guard. Is the work you speak of for her majesty?"

Aidan didn't look at him but faced forward not wanting to rattle the old man. "What concern is it of yours, old man?"

The old man motioned to the bartender to bring him a mug of ale. The bartender brought him one and left as if on cue to clear some tables.

Aidan tried again. "I ask because I heard rumors Simon moved shop. He feared the queen's guard closing in on him. I am Sir Aidan of Alange and in the guard. I just finished of my daily duty hence the uniform. You must believe me. I have no intention of harming the blacksmith. I ask because I need to protect someone from the queen. Someone I love more than life itself."

The old man studied him taking in his obvious woeful demeanor before he answered. "Son, my name is Allen. I have observed your mannerisms. You strike me as sincere and in deep emotional turmoil, but I need to know more about this woman you love. Is she in danger?"

"Yes, from Alasdair, the queen's wizard. If you can help me, I will pay you whatever you ask for that information. I will do anything. She has less than a week's time before they kill her. Please, I beg of you. I need to consult with Simon."

The old man remained cautious. "Tell me, young knight, how did you hear of Simon?"

"From talk in the castle walls between the other guards who curse him daily for helping political prisoners escape."

The old man paused. "How do I know you're sincere?"

Aidan looked the man in the eyes. "If any from my guard knew I spoke with you about seeking help for my love, I would be executed for treason without even the smallest thought of a trial. I have as much to lose as you do. I hope I can trust you with my life as well."

It was obvious to Aidan this old man had listened to many pleas for help. He said he believed him and identified himself as Simon's scout priding himself on separating the true from the trickery. He recognized the deep pain in his eyes.

"All right then lad, I can see pain in your eyes and hear it in your voice. You strike me as most sincere. Simon moved deeper into the forest making him more difficult to reach. Come meet me out back of the pub. We can talk more in private. I will leave first. Wait five minutes before you follow."

The old man stood, put some coin down on the bar and left. Aidan took his time drinking the rest of his ale so as not to arouse suspicion. He looked around at the patrons who were all in heated conversations and too involved to notice his departure. Aidan placed coin on the counter and left walking around the back of the stone building looking for Allen.

"Psst. I'm over here behind the shed."

Aidan looked around to make sure he was not being followed. Allen signaled again from behind the shed. Aidan walked over and listened to his concern.

"Trust me, son. We have helped many. I will tell you Simon's whereabouts but you must swear on your life that you will keep it secret."

Aidan raised his hand. "I swear on my life."

"Good. You must leave your horse here before walking through the field across the road until you reach the forest. Once inside the forest, you will go west a hundred paces until you come to a large oak marked with white paint. From that point, go south eighty paces before heading west for another hundred. Once that far along, you will see his white cottage with a thatched roof covered in vines. The vines give the cottage the appearance of being part of the forest.

"When you find Simon, you must call out to him that I, Allen, sent you before you approach. Tell him you are in trouble and seek his help in a matter of the heart or he will shoot you with his bow. He's a skilled marksman, you know. No need to pay me. Save your money for what may come later.

Grateful, he shook Allen's trembling hand.

"Thank you, kind sir. On my honor as a knight, I am in your debt. I have to ask one more favor of you. Please tell no-one of our conversation."

Allen moved his hand across his face as if to seal his lips shut. "Your request is safe with me."

Aidan remained curious wanting to know more. "Is it true that if Simon can't help prove a prisoner's innocence, he sends him out of the country? I know the queen, since Alasdair's appointment, has made hunting down Simon a priority. She fears the dissidents' plot to overthrow her. The more I learn about Simon, the more respect I have for him, in secret of course. I could be tried for treason just speaking these very words."

"Son, your words are music to this old man's ears. What you heard is true. Your words are safe with me or we both shall meet the same fate."

Aidan bowed before walking to the front of the pub. An adept warrior, he wanted to make sure he was not being followed.

He stopped and looked around once more before stepping off the narrow path and walking through the open field. When he reached the entrance to the forest, he began to count steps. It was late afternoon, almost dusk, making it easier for him to disappear into the darkness of the trees. Once he lost sight of the village, he sped up turning at the large oak. Weary, the smell of smoke encouraged him. Though he was tired, he kept a fast pace through the thick vines and flora, believing Simon was not far away.

Aidan soon learned he was right. Two large black barking dogs ran into the brush toward him. He jumped back. The two dogs held their stance keeping him at bay. A man heeding his dogs' warning stepped out from his stable holding a lit torch in one hand. It was dusk. Aidan could see horses grazing in an open patch of field next to the stable. There was a small cottage nearby with a thatched roof. The man lifted his torch to get a better look at Aidan before calling out.

"Who goes there?" Pulling a large knife from his belt with his other hand, the man listened for a reply.

"It is I, Sir Aidan of Alange, guard to her majesty the queen. My father was the town baker. I come regarding a personal matter of the heart and not as a threat. I am desperate for your help. Allen sent me. Please hear me out before you pass hasty judgment and kill me."

A few seconds of silence passed before the man spoke. "Why do you come so late in the day? Explain yourself before I carve you up to feed my pigs."

Aidan knelt down and raised his arms in the air to demonstrate he meant no harm.

"Kind sir, the love of my life is being held hostage by Alasdair and the queen. They want to perform some magic experiment on her to make the queen younger by draining my love of her youth and hence life. I have less than one week to rescue her. I hope to leave the country with her to protect her. Please help me. I will pay whatever you demand. I am begging on my knees."

Aidan bowed his head again.

The man proceeded with caution. "Drop the sword on your belt, knight."

Aidan did as he asked. The blacksmith hesitated a few minutes until he felt it safe to continue. Once he did, he motioned for Aidan to stand and come closer.

Aidan obliged walking out of the shadows with both hands in the air. The man looked strong and muscular. Aidan guessed he was sixty since he had more gray hair than brown. The rugged face bore the wrinkles and scars of a long life.

"Keep those hands in the air. If you are lying to me, I'll have to kill you. Prove to me you are who you say."

"Look at my crest. My coat of arms."

The man took a few steps closer and squinted at the crest. He appeared satisfied.

"Leave your sword on the ground and come to me so I can feel for any other weapons."

Aidan obliged pulling his own dagger from his boot and throwing it over to his feet. The man moved in and patted him down.

"Except for those two weapons, you're clean. Now come inside where we can talk without fear of killing each other. I'm Simon."

Relieved, Aidan agreed and followed the blacksmith inside the cottage. He was surprised to see how cozy his home was. The cottage consisted of one large room with a hearth as a stove, a log table with benches and a bed. His wife, a full figured middle-aged woman, greeted us at the door. Her cheeks flushed when he entered. She appeared aghast at a queen's guard in uniform in her house. She must have feared for her husband's safety not to mention her own.

"Marie, please be so kind as to make the young lad some tea. His name is Aidan and his father was our village baker. No need for fear. The matter needing our assistance is of the heart. I'm sure you'll be in complete sympathy."

Marie, looking somewhat less frightened, nodded, and offered me some motherly advice. "You poor lad, love is more difficult than our poets make it seem. I'll have some tea for you soon."

"Thank you. I appreciate your kindness. There's no place else I can turn."

With that, Marie put the kettle on the fire before stirring a large pot next to it. He sat down at the log table beside Simon.

"Now Sir Aidan, let's start at the beginning."

"What I am about to say is the truth. I swear on my father's grave. I guard and fell in love with the future queen."

Aidan saw his statement puzzled Simon.

"Has the queen struck ill? Probably poisoned by her own policies for the little people?"

Aidan shook his head. "No this was a scheme concocted by her wizard, Alasdair."

Simon showed no surprise at that. He shuddered at the mere mention of the wizard's name.

"A nasty man that. Alasdair is the reason we're in hiding. I put new hooves on one of the castle guards' horses. The guard did not feed that magnificent animal properly. I reminded him of that, often sneaking the horse some hay myself. One day he rode that horse hard. The animal collapsed and died. The guard told Alasdair it was my workmanship that caused the accident and not his lack of care. Of course, that evil wizard believed his guard and put a bounty on my head for my arrest and execution.

"I convinced Marie that we should go into hiding and help others wrongly accused as we had been. She knew the risks. We have to move often. We now live by the kindness of those I help, and swear to help anyone wrongly accused by Alasdair and the queen."

Aidan was in complete sympathy. "Sorry for your trouble, Simon. That wizard is pure evil. Alasdair told her majesty he Traveled to the future and found her future relative who bears the exact resemblance of her highness as a young woman. That relative is named Danielle and is the woman I love. She is much younger than the queen. Alasdair promised the queen to give Danielle's youth to her majesty while killing my love in the process. He further told the queen that she would enjoy eternal youth. The wizard then asked that he could be her first lover once the procedure was complete."

Simon glanced over at Marie who blushed, saying, "Oh my."

The blacksmith shook his head. "Just when I thought I had heard everything. When will all this happen?"

Marie carried a tray with two chipped china cups and an old porcelain teakettle to the table before the knight answered Simon. She poured two cups of tea.

"He said within a week. He has to get some potions ready as well as some samples from the young lady and the queen. He has to keep my Danielle healthy until then."

"Less than a week? That's difficult even for a plotting soul such as me. What are your thoughts? Are you planning to take her to a safe place before returning hoping not to be identified, or is your wish as you mentioned to leave and stay with her?"

"She is the love of my life. I cannot bear the thought of living without her. I have no other family. Of course, I will stay with her wherever she goes."

"I see. You realize once the queen notices your absence, you will be a marked man. She will send all of her men after the two of you. That makes this most difficult. Sip your tea while I think. Marie, do we have any more of your delicious biscuits, and is that lamb stew I smell?"

Marie grinned and said, "Why yes, dear. I'll fetch you both some."

Marie left and Simon's eyes lit up. He leaned in closer.

"All right. Here's what I think. To be out of range of the queen's men, you must leave France and the continent. I must get you to the coast and arrange for you to board an English trade ship. It will be costly, not for my services but for the British captain to sneak you aboard. I'll contact the one I trust the most. I will not lie to you, son. It's the most risky of all the plans. It's a fifty- fifty shot you make it to England alive. If the queen's men don't kill you first, the sea this time of year will do so easily. Do you understand the pitfalls? Are you sure you wouldn't prefer something safer that will keep you in France hidden by our contacts, but always on the run."

"Simon, I understand the risks. I have no choice but to leave France if Danielle and I are to stay together. Always on the run is not a life I want for us. I have some money saved. How much do you think the English captain will charge?"

"Around two hundred francs."

"That's most all of my life savings but I'll do it. Now tell me how we start?"

Before Simon could answer, Marie served hot biscuits and stew.

"Lad, first I'll need to loan you a horse. You can't ride one from the queen's stable because they are too easy to recognize. I hope your lady is a good rider. The path to the coast is an easy three-day ride from dawn to dusk. I will pre-arrange three stops to safe houses before reaching your last destination.

"Each village will have one of our contacts ready and trained to assist you. Your contact will supply you with a map to the next stop and the symbols that mark their signs. When you reach the third village, you will be near the coast. There you will leave the horse with your guide. At that point, the guide will lead you as close to your ship as possible.

"We are a chain of brothers in arms against unlawful imprisonment and executions. We have helped dozens in trouble with the monarchy. You will have lodging, food, and clothes provided at each stop."

"It pleases me your plan is so well-organized," Aidan said. "I cannot tell you how much I appreciate your help. I feel better about proceeding. Your plan appears reasonable. How can I ever repay you?"

"Sir Aidan, you put a smile on my face by just saying that. You can't repay me. I do it out of kindness and fairness. With the conditions in our country such as they are, any one of us could share your same fate. When you are properly settled, please provide an act of kindness for someone else in trouble."

Aidan wanted to show Simon his gratitude so he removed his heavy gold ruby ring.

"Please, take this. It is very valuable. The queen herself gave it to me for bravery in battle. Buy your Marie a new frock and another horse for yourself. I will return the act of kindness but I wish to do something for both of you now."

Simon valued his cause more than worldly possessions. He refused to take the ring.

Aidan took Simon's weathered hand, opened it, and placed the ring in his palm. "Please take it," he pleaded.

Simon shrugged his shoulders. "I expect nothing for what I do. It pleases me to help others who face the same fate I did. Thank you. You are a kind, generous young man. The money that comes from your ring will help another."

Aidan touched Simon's shoulder. "And you are a caring generous savior to those of us in distress. Please, sir, when will you be ready for us?"

"Give me three days to alert those with whom you will stay. I will send my messenger pigeons out tonight. Remember your most important task is to get the both of you out of the castle safely and here on that third day so we can begin. Take this note with you."

Simon was still seated when he picked up a quill pen and a very small piece of parchment. He wrote some notes down quickly before folding the paper and handing it to Aidan.

"Go here and ask for this man tomorrow after your guard duty. He will be the key to your escape from the castle. By the time you return here with Danielle, I will have your map, directions, and signs ready."

Aidan bowed. "I must return to the castle before I am missed. I will read your note in private. Thank you again, kind sir."

Aidan stood and shook Simon's hand before turning to Marie and bowing. She gave him a hug. Aidan left walking back to where he dropped his weapons. He picked them up before counting his steps into the darkness of the forest and back to his horse still tied to the pub's hitching post in the village. Once he tended to his horse, Aidan stopped next door at the bakery to buy some bread before continuing to the castle. He hoped that would make him appear like any other knight off duty, in need of strong ale, a willing wench, and a good loaf. Once composed, Aidan headed back to the castle.

Riding over the castle bridge, Aidan held his loaf up high. His cohorts laughed and waved him across unaware of the enormous burden Aidan carried in his heart. He remained cautious entering the castle about a half an hour before the start of his guard duty, a typical time for knights on leave. Once back inside, he cleared his mind, changed his uniform, and greeted his fellow workers before attending to his duty.

# Chapter Five

"I deliver your breakfast tray, my lady," Aidan called through the door.

I welcomed the sound of his voice more than he could imagine. "Yes, please come in."

I opened the door for him. He placed the tray on the table before closing and locking my door. Placing his fingers over his lips, he signaled for me to remain quiet as he began to tell me about the resisters.

"My love, I have news of our escape, but I must speak fast and in whispers. We both know these walls may have evil ears listening. I have a plan for three days hence. It is risky and not with guaranteed success, but it is our best escape route if we plan to stay together. While you eat your breakfast, I will tell you everything so as not to arouse suspicion."

Aidan told me how he had found Simon and the plan they formed. I would accept any risk to live my life with him.

After finishing his story, he took my hand. "Danielle, my heart was filled with the hope that we could be together in safety."

I finished my breakfast wanting to hear more of Aidan's story. He sensed that. "I have more to tell you, but we must remain discreet."

Aidan went over to the door and peered out. "It's still all clear. I will stand guard for a short while. Call me back inside to pick up your tray so I can tell you the rest."

I waited a good ten minutes before opening the window on my door.

"Guard, please remove my tray. While you are inside, I have a drawer that's stuck shut."

Aidan flashed me a smile. "Yes my lady" as he stepped back inside.

He began to speak as soon I closed the door.

* * * *

About ten minutes after Aidan left my room that morning, my bedroom door burst open as if pushed by a strong wind. That wind carried Alasdair, holding a suspicious leather satchel. He glared at me in a most disturbing manner before greeting me in his usual snarky manner. I hated the sound of his miserable voice so much I wanted to cover my ears.

"Hello, my lovely princess. Don't look so upset. You'll only crease that beautiful face of yours with frown lines. Very soon, you will be queen, and I will be the first in line to taste your charms. However, for today, I need to perform a few tests."

A few tests? What torture did he have in store now?

Alasdair approached the bed, placing his ominous black satchel on the night table. He opened it removing a pair of the longest sharpest scissors I have ever seen. He stared at me.

"Come, my sweet. Please come sit on this straight chair."

I refused at first, but decided to do as he said. I had no one to protect me and I could not counteract his spells. Alasdair held my arm as I stepped onto the footstool and walked over to the chair. I could hear him snapping that nasty pair of scissors behind me.

They were long, thin like a surgeon's tool, with sharp blades at each end. I cringed wondering what he was going to do to me, but put on a brave face not wanting Alasdair to have the satisfaction of knowing he was frightening me. He separated a swatch of my hair.

"Good, now that you are seated, lean forward so I can cut this bit of your hair. That's all I need."

I tried to rise and leave, but he grabbed me by my arm and forced me to sit. Alasdair's grasp was so strong I knew bruises would result.

"Stay. This entire process can go smoothly or I can make it the most difficult and painful day of your life."

Scared silly, I stayed still. He clipped hair from the side of my face and wrapped it in thin paper. I panicked in silence as I watched him take out a thin short knife.

"Now let me have your arm."

My arm? What did he want with my arm?

I refused to cooperate. He became agitated and pulled my arm toward him so hard I sensed another bruise forming. Alasdair took the small sharp knife and scraped skin from my forearm, wrapping it separately from the swatch of my hair. He put the knife back only to remove a long thin needle from his bag. He poked my finger catching the small drops of blood in a glass container. I looked away, bruised and sore from the scraping and poking.

Alasdair sneered at me. "You did well, my sweet. I think I have enough to work with, but if I do not, I can always come back for more. Now once I combine my herbs and potions with your samples and the queen's, I'll see if we can make you queen sooner than anticipated. I can't wait to feel your young body. I hungered for you when I first saw you in my thoughts. Danielle, you are a desirable woman."

He took my hand. To my surprise, his hot touch did not burn my skin. My stomach turned just being so close to him. I hated him so much I spit in his face.

"Don't celebrate yet, Alasdair. Your ugly wart-filled body will never touch mine. Not a chance. Not as long as I have any breath left." I pulled my hand out of his.

He laughed. "Feisty aren't we. I always liked my women to have spirit. More of a challenge, but one way or another, I always win. When I'm finished with you, you won't have any breath left."

Alasdair released the most evil laugh I ever heard. I refused to let him see my fear and spit in his face again. His eyes glowed blood red before he turned to leave.

"We'll see how brave you are when I start the procedure. Goodbye for now, my lovely. I can't wait to hold you in my arms and show you all of my deepest desires."

With that, he left me alone to my thoughts.

I barely caught my breath from my visit with Alasdair when Aidan returned with afternoon tea. He was a welcome sight. Once he was safely inside my room, he placed the tea tray down on the table before locking the door.

I hugged him and blurted out my bad news. "Aidan, Alasdair was here and hopes to complete the procedure earlier than expected. Please tell me more about the plan. I need to know if our escape is viable."

Aidan sighed. "At first I was having doubts about Simon's plan. I debated mentally if it was too risky."

I needed to know. "My love, are there any other options?"

Aidan shook his head. "No. I asked Simon to tell me everything about the plan. I said I wanted to make this decision carefully though I realized this may be our only way out. I trusted Simon had dealt with enough people in trouble to understand my feelings. Of course, he obliged. Now we must prepare ourselves for an arduous journey."

\* \* \* \*

Alasdair trusted Aidan because my knight did everything the wizard asked of him. That's why he was chosen to be my guard. I love Aidan but I remained torn between wanting to come home to Naples and keeping him in my life. I put my teacup down once he finished revealing the entire plan.

"What's expected of me again?"

"Remember, Simon gave me his word that he would arrange for a horse to take us to three key villages before making our way to the coast. There, we will board a pre-arranged ride on a trade ship to England. Once out of France, the queen's authority becomes null. I never asked, but you do ride, I hope?"

"Yes, yes I do. I'm a member of a riding stable at home, but won't the queen send her men after us?"

"Of course, she needs you for the spell. She will send every available guard to hunt us down. Unfortunately, this is our only option to stay together."

'Only option' resonated in my ears. That thought alone scared the heck out of me.

Aidan walked over and got down on his knees, took my hand, and kissed it. "Danielle, I love you with all my heart. Would you rather I rode you to safety and you left to board the ship alone? I cannot bear that thought."

To be honest, I couldn't bear that thought either. He'd been my rock, my lover, my friend. My gut cringed with pain at the awful realization that I wouldn't be getting home anytime soon if at all. I thought about my mother, my cat Surfer, and my store. Mom was on vacation right now, but if I wasn't there when she returned, she would be worried sick. Last but not least, there was my store. It's what I do and defines who I am. I left it closed with no sign of reopening. I realized my life would never be the same.

What if I never returned? Who would take care of everything? What would my friends and family think? They might spend the rest of their lives searching for me. As those thoughts raced through my mind, I looked into Aidan's eyes and said the words we both needed to hear.

"Of course I want us to be together. I want that more than anything."

Aidan stood and helped me rise from the chair. He put his muscular arms around my waist, pulling me toward him. He leaned down kissing my lips ever so gently. Our soft kiss soon turned passionate.

"I must leave now, my love, before someone becomes suspicious. Stay in this mood. I have been ordered to return with your supper."

My body desired him. My heart longed for his love.

I tried to stay busy until supper. That wasn't hard. Alasdair blew in again to torment me saying he needed another clipping of my hair. He cut more strands and left.

Sometime later, there was a gentle knock. "May I serve your supper, my lady?"

I opened the door eager for Aidan's touch. He placed the tray on the table and pulled me close to him.

"Danielle, I need to feel your love. I must leave at the end of my guard duty to finalize our escape plan."

We stood there for a few minutes holding each other as tight as we could. We became lost in our love and frozen in time. Aidan slowly walked us back to the bed and helped me up.

Looking longingly into my eyes, he kissed my lips tenderly moving his kisses down my neck and onto my shoulders. I eagerly helped him undo my bodice and slid my skirt off. I couldn't think straight. All I knew was how much I wanted him. I didn't care if Alasdair burst in that second. We lay there enjoying passionate pleasures totally oblivious to the dangers that lay ahead of us. After our lovemaking, we held each other like tomorrow would never come.

Aidan kissed me and whispered, "My love, I must leave you now. After my duty, I will learn more about our escape, but I will not see you until tomorrow. Now hurry, we must dress in case Alasdair lurks nearby."

With that, he stood and put on his uniform. He helped me off the bed and I dressed as quickly as I could before going to the mirror to fix my hair and lip rouge. Aidan kissed me on the cheek and left with my tray. Our timing was impeccable because fifteen minutes hadn't passed before my door burst open again with a disturbed Alasdair stomping in unannounced.

## Chapter Six

The next day, Aidan, while waiting for his guard duty to end, spoke patiently with everyone, handling all their requests while staying later than expected in order not to arouse suspicion. Once off duty, Aidan walked to his horse. He remained calm and steady as he mounted his steed and rode over the drawbridge. He did not pick up speed until he was out of the other guards' sights.

When he felt far enough way, Aidan stopped to read Simon's directions.

Simon wrote that Aidan needed to find an old monastery hidden deep in the thickest part of the forest. Aidan followed Simon's exact directions, guiding his horse down dirt roads and up green tree lined hills. At a certain point, Aidan would see smoke and a group of structures would come into his view.

When they did, Aidan walked his horse toward the group of four gray stone cottages with a small chapel at their center. Two large barns completed the complex. Multi colored wildflowers lined the entrance.

Aidan watched as some of the brothers tended to their vegetable garden while others gathered around a wooden cart hitched to a donkey. He marveled at how well the monks fared being so far from the village.

Simon had written that the monks who worshipped here were noted for their wonderful sparkling wines, a thought that brought a smile to Aidan's tired face. Sparkling wines were reserved only for the rich and royal.

Aidan tied his horse to a post near the entrance to the first stone building. An elderly monk with a long white beard and, using an old branch for a walking stick, limped over to him carrying some hay for Aidan's horse under one arm.

"Welcome, my son. Welcome to the Brothers of Aloire. I am Brother Theo. Your horse looks weary so I brought him some nourishment. I'll have one of the younger monks bring him a bucket of water. You look weary as well. How may we assist your soul once we have replenished your body?"

Aidan bowed out of respect. He studied Theo's wrinkled skin and bald head when the old monk's hood dropped to his shoulder.

"Your order's kindness, Brother, is legendary. I appreciate your hospitality. I am tired from my journey, but my concern is a matter of the heart. I have been instructed to seek the assistance of Brother Louis. Do you know where I might find him?"

Aidan watched as Brother Theo grinned from ear to ear. Simon indicated that Brother Louis had a very unconventional reputation.

"Yes, son, I do, but if your dilemma regards matters of the heart no matter how difficult, I am just as suited to advise you."

"I appreciate your offer, kind sir, but my contact insisted I had to speak to Brother Louis."

The wise old monk turned and pointed to the donkey cart Aidan saw when he first arrived. "I see. It must be a very unusual request. Brother Louis has a special talent for those. He is the tall monk over there in front of the grape press. We just brought some sparkling wine up from the cave. It has been riddled. If you're lucky, Brother Louis might offer you a taste once the bottles are loaded for delivery to the castle."

Aidan thanked the old monk again and headed toward the grape press. He spotted the tall, muscular, middle-aged monk instructing the younger ones. He stood in a line from the cave to the cart.

"Careful, Samuel, don't try to pass too many bottles at once. You easily could drop one leaving us short for the queen's cellar."

Aidan watched young Samuel put down the extra bottle passing one bottle at a time to load in the specially built box on the back of the cart.

He called out hoping Brother Louis would hear him. "Brother Louis. Simon sent me. I am the Aidan he contacted you about and beg for some of your time."

The monk turned around when Aidan finished speaking and looked at him with his sun weathered and scarred face. "Ah yes. Sir Aidan. A talented carrier pigeon advised me you would be coming to seek my advice. Let me finish my task here and we will go to a more private place suited for such conversations. I may even open a bottle for you to taste. Once we have finished loading, it is our custom to share a sample."

Aidan bowed out of respect to the monks and their service. "I would be honored to wait for you. I appreciate your time and would be delighted to taste your legendary wine."

Aidan watched as the last bottle was loaded. Brother Louis waved to two of the young monks standing near the front of the cart.

"Now go. Be careful. These forests paths are bumpy. We don't want to lose any of the bottles. The queen's guard will send back some vegetables from her majesty's garden and meat from the guards' hunt. Go on. What are you waiting for?"

The two monks climbed up to the seats in the front of the cart and one gave the donkey a quick whip before waving good-bye and leaving. With his eye, Brother Louis followed them all the way to the entrance gate.

"Ah, by now the other brothers have scattered with the extra bottles but were thoughtful enough to leave one here for us. They took five of six to sample, but one is all we need. Come with me."

Aidan followed the monk from the cart's departure point down a short hill to the entrance of the cave. Brother Louis grabbed two tin cups sitting next to the entrance and handed them to Aidan. He turned from the cave's entrance to enter a humble stone building next to it. Inside, he walked behind a decorated altar before entering a dark narrow hallway lit by torches.

Brother Louis carried the bottle of wine in one hand while motioning with the other for Aidan to go through a doorway that led to a closet sized room with no windows and no light. Brother Louis then removed one of the torches from the hallway and lit a big round ivory candle centered on a round wooden table carved from a tree trunk that took up most of the room. Two log benches served as seats.

Aidan sat down on one, placing the two cups in the center of the table. Brother Louis returned the torch to its proper place before coming back and sitting across from him. Aidan remained silent.

Brother Louis broke the silence. "Ah this is the day I wait for each year. The first tasting."

The strong monk put the bottle of sparkling wine down on the table before reaching in his pocket to pull out a small long sharp knife. He carefully placed the thin blade between the bottle's edge and the cork pulling it slowly to pop the cork. The golden bubbly liquid poured out and Brother Louis filled their cups.

"I know my fellow brothers in the Champagne monastery think their sparkling wines are better than ours. They have made some for His Holiness, the Pope. Our grapes are well suited for sparkling wine. I imagine this would taste better in the queen's crystal, but for now, try some in one of our tin mugs. I promise you won't be disappointed."

Brother Louis handed Aidan one of the cups. Aidan sipped, letting the bubbly liquid gold linger in his mouth. He smiled pleased with the taste. His reaction made Brother Louis' gray eyes sparkle.

"I have never tasted anything so wonderful," Aidan said. "I know you send bottles to the castle every year, but the queen saves them for her banquet guests, her lovers, and herself. She has never shared any with her workers or guards. Thank you."

Brother Louis nodded in appreciation.

Aidan continued. "This is the best wine I have ever had. Unfortunately, I cannot savor it for long. I must deal with our business. My words are for your ears only. I beg your confidence."

"Our conversation shall remain private," Brother Louis reassured him. "You have my word as a man of the cloth. Now tell me about your situation."

Aidan poured his heart out to Brother Louis who listened with a sympathetic ear. "Danielle is the only woman I have ever loved. She is at the core of my dilemma. I have no one else in my life who loves me. My mother died at my birth. My father worked himself to death. I love Danielle and want to spend the rest of my life with her. The queen's wizard, Alasdair, has other plans. He wants to kill her to assuage the vain queen's desire to regain her youth. We are working with Simon, hoping to plot our escape."

Brother Louis interrupted. "I know firsthand how evil Alasdair can be. He influenced the queen into banishing our order deep into these woods because Alasdair feared her majesty was seeking advice from one of our brothers. He thought the queen would develop a conscience and delay the execution of one of her guards. The guard in question was innocent of disobeying the wizard's orders, but Alasdair believed the queen's romantic interest in him to be a threat to his own powerful hold on the queen. Our sparkling wine and the queen's affinity for it is the reason we remain alive.

"Of course, I will help you. I have helped many, but you must pay strict attention to my instructions. Each successful escape from the castle is unique and requires skillful planning. Each case must remain unique or the guards will know of my plans.

"In your case, we must have your young lady leave the castle grounds safely and unnoticed. She, as well as you, will need a disguise. An oversized monk's robe works well for both a man and a woman. I have some extra robes for occasions such as these. The hoods are full enough to cover her hair and face." Brother Louis stopped to sip his wine.

"You are probably wondering how I will deliver the robe to her. You will do the honors. To fool the guards, we must arrange for me to administer last rites to Danielle the day before Alasdair plans to kill her. When the time proves right, she will don her robe and leave as a monk.

"No one will suspect me of any tricks. They know I supply the queen's wine cellar and often make myself available for confessions of the guard as well as the queen's court. That group needs more than confession if they agree to carry on the wishes of Alasdair and the queen."

Brother Louis looked deep into Aidan's eyes. "Now here is the key to making this plan work. Danielle will have to ask the queen for permission to have me, and only me, hear her last confession the afternoon before her scheduled execution. She is entitled to that. Even that miserable excuse for a queen should agree.

"As I said before, I will enter the castle on the day of your escape ready for confession. We will wait for the guard change so Danielle will have to learn their schedule. Once the guards change duty, we will change into our new identities. She will leave wearing one of our robes, walking with her head down and her hands folded in front of her. She must move at a very slow pace so as not to arouse suspicion.

"I will wear the uniform of a chimney sweep under my robe and leave as such once she is safely on the other side of the bridge. You will need a robe as well. I will explain to Brother Michael who launders our robes why we need to borrow two. He will agree that they are for a worthy cause. Not one of our brothers holds any admiration for Alasdair. Please sit and enjoy the rest of your wine. I will return shortly with your robes."

Brother Louis left Aidan alone in the room for about ten minutes. He returned carrying two brown robes with a burlap sack to hold them. The monk held the robes up for Aidan to see.

"Here you go. These should work fine. Trust me. We'll be successful as long as we remain vigilant. As I said before, a monk or two visits the castle weekly for the confessions of the court. Now before you leave, let's enjoy one more cup of this extraordinary sparkling wine."

Aidan watched eager to see Brother Louis uncork the bottle again and refill their two mugs.

"Here's to your successful escape and to a long and happy life with Danielle. Here's to outwitting Alasdair and the queen."

The two men clicked their mugs and drank. When they finished, Aidan knelt for a blessing. Brother Louis obliged.

"May you both go in peace and may your love endure."

Aidan stood, picked up the sack, and thanked the selfless monk before taking his leave. "I hope I will be able to return your kindness one day."

Brother Louis walked Aidan to his horse. He headed back to the castle wondering if this plan would succeed and if Danielle had remained safe during his absence.

# Chapter Seven

I believed Aidan would have everything under control, but I wavered with Alasdair staring me in the face. That nasty excuse for a man entered my room unannounced again.

"Why my lovely future queen, you're flushed. You must be happy to see me. I'm happy to see you as I contemplate our future together."

He moved his tongue to wet his bluish lips. "If only you knew how much I long to kiss you."

His eyes glowed. His face grew red. He came close enough to touch me. I shuddered at the thought as he reached out.

"However, for now, I need to take some final measurements. Odd, I should have left without them last time. I must have wanted to see your beautiful green eyes again."

I didn't want any part of his plan for final measurements. I tried to dance around him. He caught me by my wrist. It burned from his touch.

"Would you prefer I call a guard to assist me?"

I shook my head, determined not to shame myself. "No".

"Good then, stand straight so I can measure your waist."

The mere thought of that man touching any part of my body filled me with disgust. Alasdair placed a tailor's tape around my waist. He measured my neck, my arm length, but worst of all, my chest. He wrote everything down in a small leather-bound notebook.

"Lovely. Remember my pretty, you heard the queen say I will be her first lover the evening of her transformation."

I wanted to scream at him "No way," but I just smiled hoping Aidan would return with good news about our escape.

Alasdair glanced up at me from his notebook. "Oh how careless of me. I forgot to mention this. Did I tell you the queen is so excited about the progress of her impending transformation, we are moving the scheduled procedure up two days? We shall be together sooner than I expected. That alone should provide you with wonderful dreams tonight."

Nightmares more likely.

He placed his head back and cackled before turning and leaving. He departed so fast, it was as if he vanished into a thin trail of black smoke. I paced the floor most of the night wondering if Aidan would have any good news.

I couldn't wait for morning. I was stressed by Alasdair's latest news. I wanted to tell Aidan about the newest complication. When the first rays of sunlight peeked through the drapes, I leaped out of bed. I had not slept well from the thought of what might happen to me. I put my robe on as soon as I heard a strong knock on the door.

It was Aidan. His reassuring voice comforted me. "Good morning, my lady. I know it's early, but I have your breakfast tray."

I opened the door. My knight rushed in putting the tray down on the table. I shot him a serious look.

"You are early, my love, but I'm grateful to see you. Alasdair visited me yesterday to take my measurements and inform me he moved the procedure up two days. I don't know what to do. That gives us even less time."

Aidan looked concerned, but comforted me. "Danielle, do not worry. Sit and have your breakfast. You must eat to keep your strength up for our journey. I will tell you more about our escape plan as you do."

He held the chair for me and I sat down to eat my breakfast. Aidan sat across from me. I could sense how nervous he was.

"Listen to me very carefully. I have to make sure you are up to what is expected of you if we are to succeed. First, I visited Brother Louis yesterday at his monastery. He's one of Simon's oldest friends and advisors. Alasdair banished his entire order of monks to the forest for trying to dissuade the queen from executing one of her own guards."

That fact didn't shock me. Alasdair had a nasty habit of doing horrid things to anyone who crossed him.

"Danielle that wizard has more power than you or I can ever imagine. Listen. Please, just listen to me. On the day of our escape, Brother Louis wants you to disguise yourself as a monk. On that day, he will visit your room to hear your confession, which you must prearrange with the queen. Once the guards shift duty, you will leave in his place and he will depart as a chimney sweep. The guard schedule should remain the same unless Alasdair decides to change it. The kind monk sent me off with two monk's robes, one for each of us.

"Our escape will be two days from today. That should give us enough time even with Alasdair's new timetable. The night before we are to leave, I will hide your robe in a covered dish and deliver it with your dinner. You must request today to see Brother Louis for confession on the afternoon of our escape. I doubt if the queen would deny you that.

"Once Brother Louis is here with you, you must wait for the guard change before donning the robe and pulling the hood down over your face as far as it will go. You will then go in silence. If someone asks a question, just nod without looking up or answering. Your actions will not appear odd. Many monks in Brother Louis' order take a vow of silence.

"Once you have left, Brother Louis will hide in your closet and wait long enough for us to leave the palace grounds. He will wear the uniform of a chimney sweep under his robe. After throwing soot on himself and his clothes from your hearth, he will leave explaining to the guard that he started work before the guard change began."

"Remember, wait for the guard change. That way no one will notice the difference in size between you and Brother Louis. Walk slowly with your head down and your hands folded just as the monks do. Have the sleeves cover your hands so no one will notice you are a woman.

"Once you have walked over the bridge and are off castle grounds look for me on horseback. I will be wearing a monk's robe. I will help you on and you will ride with me. Our escape is planned to take place right before dinner. Ask the queen if Brother Louis can hear your confession in late afternoon. I have the morning duty that day, so I will already be relieved of duty. You realize if they have any hint that it's you under that robe, they will turn you over to Alasdair on the spot."

Aidan continued. "Once I pick you up, we will ride deep into the forest to Simon's. He will meet us with a map and instructions and let us spend the first night with him. The next day we begin our journey to the coast. Simon believes it to be a four-day and three-night journey. By the fourth day, we should be able to reach our ship. Are you sure you are up to all this?"

Tears streamed down my cheeks. He spoke in normal phrases but the facts spun around in my brain like a child's top. I needed to rant my frustrations out loud to him.

"What ship? Who's Simon? Who's Brother Louis? I have to trust my life to total strangers. What choice do I really have? Do we have? It's the only way we can stay together. Oh how I wish I sent Alasdair to another store with that dagger. I wish I never met him."

Aidan took my hand. "But then I would have never met you, my love."

I looked into his eyes. His stare melted my heart.

"Yes. You are so right. I fell in love with you the first time I saw you. I will do this, even though it scares me to death. I'll do it for us."

I sobbed, which was unlike me. I've always been able to hold it together, no matter what the problem. Aidan held me, trying to comfort me after that difficult acceptance of reality.

"Calm down, Danielle. We will be fine. I know it. I won't let anything happen to you."

I wiped my eyes. His inner strength gave me peace.

"Are you better now?"

I nodded.

"Good. My love, please remember the day Brother Louis comes for confession, you are to wear light clothes like one of the castle maids. No fancy gowns. Braid your hair and wear it up tight. No rouge or rosewater for fragrance in case you walk close by any of the guards. I will sneak you in a pair of men's scandals when I deliver the robe so your walk will appear masculine.

"None of my fellow guards know of our plan. I trust no one, only Simon, his contacts, and Brother Louis. Any of those guards would be only too happy to turn us in or kill us so they could attain a higher rank and more influence with Alasdair. You must trust no one, my love, except for me and of course Brother Louis. Understand?"

I nodded in agreement. "Yes. Two days from now. When should I send the queen a request for confession again?"

"Send a note to the queen tonight after I am off duty. That will give the good monk enough time to plan. We will talk again later."

I kissed his cheek, thankful for all his efforts. Aidan picked up my tray and left. I sat there with my head in my hands wondering if we would ever escape the castle safely.

He said we would talk again later. I wondered when that would be but hadn't asked. Soon after he left, Jacqueline came to my room to dress me. Once she finished, I asked for some royal stationery and a pen so I might send a special request to her majesty.

"Yes, my lady. I will find you some."

She curtsied and left, returning in a few minutes with what I needed. The stationery was elegant with gold leaf and embossed flowers. She also brought a quill pen and inkwell.

Once in a blue moon, being an antique dealer comes in handy and this was one of those peculiar times. I've written invitations to charity fundraisers and auctions with a quill pen. I thanked Jacqueline and sat at the small table in my room mentally composing this potentially life-saving document to the queen. I knew what I'd like to tell her, but that wouldn't get me very far so I began:

*Your Royal Highness, Queen Katherine,*

*As your humble servant, I am requesting an audience with a local monk from the order of Aloire for the purpose of confessing and cleansing my soul in preparation for our appointed procedure. The monk I request is Brother Louis and I request this appointment one day before our procedure in the afternoon before dinner. I appreciate your granting my dying wish and hope you understand the concern for my well-being in the hereafter as well as for your continued health.*

*Your humble servant,*
*Danielle deForet*

I sealed the letter with wax before ringing the bell for my guard. I asked him to find Jacqueline. He did and she returned shortly.

"Please deliver my letter to the queen and wait in case she has an answer for me."

"I will my lady, but you realize that everything you say or write to the queen has to be approved by Alasdair first."

I hated that man even more, but remained calm. "I'm aware of that, but show my letter to the queen first. The envelope is addressed to *Her Majesty, the Queen—A Personal Request*. Let her decide if she should show it to Alasdair or if she will make her own decision on its contents. Hide it in your skirt where it will not be seen."

Jacqueline did as I asked. When she returned, she told me the queen took the letter and muttered that she did not feel it necessary to run such a simple request by Alasdair. For once, I believed our plan might actually be put into motion. I didn't expect to hear from the queen that same day, but hoped she would grant my request by the day of our escape.

Time passed in slow motion that day. Jacqueline returned before noon with no decision. "Queen Katherine has not yet given me a response. It is time for your bath, my lady."

I followed her into the bathroom and disrobed before getting into the tub. She sprinkled rose petals on the water and helped me scrub. She knew it was her job to make me look like the future queen. She shampooed my hair before handing me a scented towel.

I stepped out of the tub and into the turquoise silk-brocade dressing gown she held for me. It felt so free, so cool, the silk so soft against my naked body that I decided to keep it on for a while. She brushed my long hair before laying out my clothes on the bed. She asked if I needed anything else before she left. I didn't.

My body felt so free without all the hoops, stays, and jewelry. I enjoyed remaining comfortable for a while. I sat on my bed daydreaming about how I'd love to see Aidan right now.

What was that? Someone knocked? Who could that be? It was too early for dinner. I soon heard Aidan's deep voice.

"My lady, I bring you afternoon tea, special complements of her majesty the queen. May I enter?"

I jumped up to answer the door. "Yes. Thank you."

Because I wasn't clothed, I opened the door just wide enough for Aidan to enter. I quickly closed it behind him, hoping he'd stay and spend some time with me.

Aidan placed a French china platter with the beautifully arranged treats on the table before pouring a cup of tea. The china was a different pattern of Limoges.

If circumstances were different, I would dig into those colorful sugary macaroons as soon as they hit the table before making a low offer on the Limoges for my shop. As I leaned over to get a better look, my robe came untied. Aidan's eyes focused on my naked body.

"Danielle. You are as lovely as one of those porcelain statues in the grand foyer, but you must cover yourself. If anyone should come in, they would kill us."

I stared into his eyes. "I may be dead soon anyway. What could be better than spending my last two days making love to you?"

He walked over and kissed me on the lips moving his wet kisses down my neck. I let go of the ties to my robe letting it drop to the floor by my feet. He stared longingly at my body.

"You are a delicate feast for my tired eyes. I love you more than life itself." He pulled me close. "Oh how I wish I knew we were safe from intruders."

"I don't care about intruders. I need to feel how much you love me."

We lay down together on the bed. I basked in the warmth and passion of his naked body against mine. His strong hands touched my skin, shifting his hands ever so gently, ever so softly to feel every part of me. My body ached with passion. I repositioned myself so he would not miss an inch. He devoured my lips before I led his kisses down my body. I could no longer control my feelings. My body burned with desire trembling at his every touch. My mind was lost in our steamy passion.

We both knew the danger of our tryst. Alasdair could walk in on us at any time. Our lovemaking was so delicious, we did not care. We were soul mates. We took a short respite before starting all over again, but our passion came to an abrupt end when we heard footsteps approach my door. We sat up to listen more intently. The footsteps did not sound like Alasdair's. We soon found out that it was Aidan's replacement. A deep male voice came through the heavy wooden door.

"Everything all right in there?"

Aidan dressed while trying to respond in a calm voice. "Yes it is. I am just removing the tea tray."

I scampered off to the commode as he picked up the tray and left. I finished dressing for fear that another unwanted visitor might appear.

## Chapter Eight

The next morning when Aidan brought my breakfast tray, he informed me he couldn't stay. "My love, forgive me, I yearn for your touch more than you know, but we must remain discreet if our plan is to work."

Every single time I glanced into those steel blue eyes, I wanted him. Yet I also wanted to escape and was smart enough to know we had to remain beyond suspicion. Our lives depended on it. I blew Aidan a kiss. He opened the door and left just as Jacqueline entered.

"Forgive me, my lady. I have orders to dress you a bit early. Have you finished your breakfast?"

"I've had enough," I answered gulping down the last few bites.

Jacqueline rushed to my closet selecting an emerald green satin gown with ruffles and bows. She dressed me before tying my hair back.

"I made these for you. I think they will look lovely in your blonde hair."

She showed me six small emerald green silk rosettes three sewn on each of two hair combs. She carefully adjusted them to each side of my head. Just as she handed me a sterling silver hand mirror, Alasdair blew in, unannounced. He rudely dismissed Jacqueline.

"You may go now maid. You did well with my little lady."

Once my maid left, Alasdair gave me the once over with his demon red eyes. "You shall meet with the queen in a short while. I will accompany you."

I walked over to the full- length mirror and did a last minute touch up to my appearance. Looking back at him through the mirror, I could see his red eyes staring at me with lust.

"You look lovely, my future queen. Now hurry. Come with me to see her majesty."

Alasdair grabbed my arm and pulled me out the door past Aidan who was talking to the guard on duty. The wizard motioned for Aidan to escort us dismissing the other guard posted by my door. Aidan followed the wizard's orders. I was relieved to have him accompany us.

We walked down the hallway and entered the throne room. Under different circumstances, I would never have tired of the room's beauty filled with a gold gilded throne, oriental carpets in blue, white, and antique vases from all over the world. The queen's maids, all young, probably in their late teens, looked beautiful in their pastel gowns. They formed a line on each side of my path up the stairs to the throne. I curtsied when I reached the top.

"Your Majesty, it is an honor to see you again."

I kept my head down even though I wanted to scream nasty things at her. I figured it best I keep my cover. I may have been angry and resentful but was not stupid. The queen glanced down at me with kindness.

"I forgot how beautiful I looked when I was your age. When I look at you, I am reminded of the happiest times of my life. I wanted to tell you in person that since you are making such a generous sacrifice on my part, I have granted your wish to meet with Brother Louis and have ordered one of my guards to inform him of such."

I breathed a deep sigh of relief hoping Aidan could hear this from his station by the doorway. From the corner of my eye, I could see Alasdair's nostrils stream black smoke. I'm sure he was angry. I went over his head. I pretended I didn't see the wizard's reaction.

I responded to the queen in a sweet voice as I curtsied, "I am indebted to your highness. Thank you. My soul needs comfort to face the sacrifice I am making in your honor."

My eyes began to tear. Easy for me to do thinking about what could happen to me if our plan didn't work. I was grateful she granted my request. She had just put our escape plan into motion. The queen walked down the steps, leaned over, and took my face in her hands.

"Look at this flawless skin. That youthful body will soon become mine. However, for today, we must meet with Alasdair for a dress rehearsal of what's to come two days hence."

Queen Katherine clapped her hands. "Prepare my way to the Rose Room."

Her maids scurried around her. One held her train while another held her hand to escort her down the stairs. The rest followed ready to act as needed. One took my hand and walked me out of the throne room staying a few paces behind the queen. Aidan threw me a quick wink as we walked past assuring me he heard that Brother Louis' visit had been approved. The women entered the Rose Room first, with Alasdair not far behind attended to by Aidan.

I looked around at the pale pink wall covering decorated with petite cherry and lavender roses on emerald green vines. The queen made her way to the front of the room and up the stairs to her cranberry velvet throne but did not sit down. She turned around to face me and clapped her hands again.

"Princess Danielle, come to me. The rest of you are dismissed. Guards remain outside the door. No one is to enter. No one is to leave until I call for you. Alasdair is the only one to remain in here with us."

I trembled. Is this a trick? It wouldn't be beneath Alasdair or the queen to start the procedure early.

I obeyed and approached the queen with caution. Alasdair took a wand out of his left sleeve. I cringed. He looked at me with anger, but did not want the queen to see him do so. He pointed the wand at the both of us, grinning before following me up the stairs.

"Danielle, face the Queen and hold both of her hands," he commanded. "Your Majesty, when we do the actual procedure, you must remove your crown because it will interfere with the magic. I need your mind to be free. Now face the princess and hold both of her hands."

The queen did as he asked. I held out both hands. Since she still had her crown on, I was relieved to think this would actually be a test run.

"Danielle, you will wear loose, light clothing like a long night dress and will wear your hair down. I shall give you some powders mixed in lavender tea to ease your pains before we begin the bodily transition.

"Your Majesty will drink a similar tea. I then hold toward the sky a gold chalice containing a combination of powdered toad and secret herbs, medicines, as well as samples of your hair, blood, and skin. Only I know the exact amounts of each.

"I will set fire to the potion, and after it has cooked and blended, I will pour it into the two cups each of you will drink at the same time. You will soon hear the swishing and grunting of the wind swirling around this room. It will pick up your inner psyches, while your bodies mesh.

"Don't either of you be afraid. The potion will make you both lose consciousness. As for you, Danielle—that may be a good thing. When the queen awakes, your majesty will be young again, while Princess Danielle will be a spirit. At that point, I will send Danielle's spirit into the afterlife accompanied by my guard bats."

The queen appeared pleased. "Thank you Alasdair."

She called out to the guards by the door. "All may enter now."

I remained quiet trying to hide my fear.

The queen clapped her hands for her maids to escort her. "You two, take the princess to her room. The rest of you escort me to the throne room."

Luckily for me, Jacqueline was at the front of the line. She took my hand and, with another maid, walked me back to my room. At this point, there was no use in trying to escape. I prayed Aidan's plan would work.

Time flew by that day. I worried I would not be convincing enough as a monk, even wearing a robe. I wondered how I could convince Jacqueline to bring me light clothes so early in the day and skip my rosewater. I might have to fake illness or distress to make the request work. A knock on the door interrupted my thoughts.

Aidan announced he was outside with my luncheon tray. I let him in, closing the door after him. He put the tray down on the table.

"My love, are you ready to see Brother Louis tomorrow? I sent a messenger pigeon to alert him. Do you remember everything required of you?"

I took his arm. "You have no idea how ready I am. Alasdair gave us a run through of what he plans to do. I will vanish into thin air if this doesn't work. Trust me. I will follow the directions exactly."

"Thin air? Is that what that monster said?"

I nodded. Tears streamed down my face.

Aidan took me in his arms. "I would have them kill me rather than let that happen to you. Trust me. Be brave my love. We will be together soon. Remember how much I love you."

With that, he kissed me before turning and leaving me alone with my thoughts.

* * * *

The much-anticipated day of our escape arrived. Too nervous to get a good night's rest, my mind bounced back and forth from our safe arrival at the coast to Alasdair. Jacqueline informed me before I retired that she would be keeping me busy most of the day with grooming requests from Alasdair and the queen. I decided to spend what little time I had writing letters to my mother including one for her to read to my precious Surfer saying good-bye and thanking both of them for their love. In my heart, I knew they would never receive them, but putting my feelings into words made me feel better and stronger to face what lie ahead. I hid the letters in my bodice when I heard a knock on the door.

It was Aidan with my breakfast tray. I opened the door and let him in. He hurried to the table and put the tray down.

"My love, I cannot stay. Please eat no matter how difficult. Who knows when we'll get a good meal again? There is one extra covered dish. Please open this one first and hide what's underneath."

He pointed to the large dish in the center of the tray, winked, and kissed my forehead. "To our future."

Aidan watched as I removed the robe and sandals from the covered dish. I stashed them under my bed behind the footstool. My brave knight opened the door ready to leave. His timing proved impeccable because Jacqueline stood at my door ready to enter. She had a surprise request for me.

"My lady, Alasdair informed me the queen requested to see you this morning. I must get you out of your robe and properly attired. Alasdair will enter soon."

I panicked. This can't be. Will he perform the procedure early?

I asked her about the visit as she helped me dress. "Please tell me, what does he want?"

Jacqueline was matter of fact. "He doesn't confide in me. I'm just her majesty's servant and he treats me as such. You, on the other hand, are the kindest royal I have ever met."

As soon as I finished dressing, I heard his dreaded footsteps. The door creaked open. I'm not exaggerating when I say that even the castle doors didn't like that man. Alasdair glared at me with his horrid red eyes.

"You are meeting with Brother Louis today. You by-passed me with your request and went straight to the queen. I demand to know why?"

I did not want to cast suspicion on our plan so I ignored his question as if it meant nothing to me. "I have no need to answer to you. The queen already approved his visit. That's all that matters."

Smoke streamed from his nostrils. "Why you insolent little wench, tell me. Now."

He grabbed my throat. His nails pierced my skin. I gasped trying to speak.

"Careful or you might damage the queen's new body."

He squeezed harder obviously not concerned that I was gagging.

I grabbed his hands to push him away choking out, "Stop. Please. I'm a religious person."

Alasdair released his grip on my throat. I fell to the floor.

"I asked the good Brother to help me pray for my soul and for the health of the queen. I want us both to fare well."

He looked down at me. "I see. You are frightened by what will happen to you?"

Tears streamed down my face. The tears were real. "Beyond belief."

In his own strange way, he tried to console me. "No need for tears. I have performed many procedures. All will be well. I have a vested interest in this, remember?"

His glance caressed me like a lecherous old man. He gave me the chills.

"Danielle, you must come with me now. We have an appointment with the queen."

He held out his arm. I was reluctant but accepted it. Once outside my room, Aidan followed. Alasdair walked me to the queen's private boudoir. He knocked politely which is more than he does for me.

"Your majesty, Danielle and I are here."

I heard her answer. "Yes. Delightful. Please come in."

Alasdair pushed me in first. I looked over at the queen's bed. She had four elegant gowns carefully placed on it. She eyeballed my figure.

"Danielle, I believe you are smaller in the waist than I. Please stand behind my dressing screen where my seamstress is waiting to take your correct measurements. After tomorrow, your measurements will be mine and I will need to have these gowns altered for the ball."

The only thing that kept me sane was our plan, so of course I obliged.

Her seamstress measured me before asking me to try on all of the dresses. I obliged, trying on each dress. After they were pinned for alterations, I walked out for the queen and her wizard to see. The queen was delighted, clapping her hands after viewing each one.

"Thank you, Danielle, They all look lovely. Very lovely, especially on you or should I say the new me. I understand Brother Louis will arrive at four this afternoon. Alasdair just told me you wanted to pray for us both. That's most kind, my dear. I will make sure Alasdair makes your spiritual journey to the afterlife as painless as possible."

I remained silent to prevent me from telling her where I wanted her to go in the afterlife and how to get there. Alasdair grabbed my arm, escorted me out of the queen's boudoir, and took me back to my room. I walked the entire way trying to avoid any eye contact with Aidan who accompanied us back.

Once inside, Alasdair closed the door rubbing his hands together. "You may fool the queen but not me. Do not try anything stupid or I will make your journey the most horrible nightmare you could ever imagine." He turned without saying another word and left followed by a haze of black smoke.

Jacqueline always checked on me in the afternoon so I thought about why I should need to change. At last, around three, she entered with fresh drinking water. I lay on the bed holding a pillow over my head in obvious discomfort.

"My lady, are you well?"

"I'm just a little light headed. Perhaps my corset is too tight."

"I am sorry if I was the cause of that. Do you wish to cancel your visit with Brother Louis?"

"No. Not at all. I would like to cancel afternoon tea and change into something less restrictive. Are there any lighter clothes that would be appropriate?"

"Why yes. The queen always keeps some peasant garments in a box on the floor of your closet. She enjoys sneaking out among us to make sure there are no plots against the throne. Sometimes it's to meet her illicit lovers. She thinks we do not know, but we hear more than she thinks. Let me unfasten your corset and I will fetch one of those dresses and cancel tea. She does have quite a few of these garments."

"Thank you. I think lighter clothes and no rosewater fragrance would make me feel better. Please keep this our secret. I need to pray with the good brother."

"I will. The secret benefits both of us. Who knows what she would do to me if she should find out I let you borrow one."

Jacqueline helped me undress, loosening the corset. I told her I felt a little better before she walked over to dig into that special box. She unlocked the closet door and pulled out a large sewing box. The queen hid her peasant clothes there. Jacqueline took a drab light gray one and held it up for my approval. I thought how perfect to wear under the monk's robe.

I nodded

"My lady, please allow me to assist you."

She dressed me so that I wore no corset or petticoats just plain undergarments. I felt free and ready for my exit.

"Let me comb your hair away from your face. That will help you feel less flushed. It's almost four."

I sat and let her tie my hair back with a ribbon. As soon as Jacqueline finished, there was a knock on the door.

The guard on duty announced,

"My lady, it's Brother Louis."

I dismissed Jacqueline asking her to let in the old monk. He entered carrying a small black leather satchel. Once my maid left and closed the door, Brother Louis turned and locked it from the inside with a key he received from Aidan on entering. He then turned his back to me and removed his robe. He wore the uniform of a chimney sweep underneath. He rolled up his robe and placed it back in the small bag.

"Danielle, you already know who I am. I feel blessed to help you and your brave knight. By now, Sir Aidan delivered a robe and sandals to you. Please find them and keep them handy. When I feel the time is right, place your robe over your dress and change your shoes."

I walked over to the footstool and moved it aside to take out the robe and sandals. I placed them on the bed ready for my change. Brother Louis then took something small out of his pocket. He held an intricately carved silver heart pendant in the air for me to see.

"I received this from Aidan when he gave me the key. He said the heart represents your love for each other and hopes that you will wear it under your robe."

Brother Louis opened the clasp and helped fasten the long chain around my neck. I held the heart thinking of Aidan and his love.

"Aidan knew you would cancel afternoon tea and felt it wise to send the necklace with me. That young man loves you with all his heart. He will do his best to make our plan work. My child, are you ready for what is to come? There will be grave danger facing the both of you."

"I am. I love Aidan. We can never be together here. My life will end. Brother Louis, thank you for your help. I will do anything you ask of me."

Brother Louis touched the top of my head. "Good. Let me bless you before you get ready to leave. Aidan said your guards change duty at half past the hour. Do they give you notice when this is about to happen?"

"Sometimes. We are in luck. Pierre is scheduled to be there now and he does announce his replacement."

The kind monk appeared pleased. "Wonderful. Now we will wait longer than you probably wish to make sure Pierre is out of the castle grounds."

Brother Louis walked over to my window.

"You have a limited view of the bridge, but we can watch him leave from here. Once he has crossed the bridge, you may start your journey. Your brave Aidan should be on his horse in the woods to the right of the bridge wearing one of our robes and waiting for you."

I was scared silly. Brother Louis sensed that. He took my hands and asked me to kneel down as he led us in prayer. He prayed for our safe journey, our health along the way, and blessed our love so that it would last a lifetime. His soothing tone made me feel calm and at peace.

Once we finished, I put the robe over my dress and fastened the scandals. I felt my hair to make sure the tie was secure. I shoved all of my hair under the back of my robe. Brother Louis pulled a vestment shawl out of his bag. I put it over my shoulders to give me more girth.

Just as we finished our preparations, Pierre announced the guard change. The kind monk looked at me sternly.

"As soon as we see Pierre cross the bridge, cover your hair and the sides of your face with the hood, walk out of this room, over the bridge and away from the palace grounds. Aidan will be waiting. He will be riding a white horse with a silver gray mane. I will remain here until I no longer see you. Since I wear the borrowed clothes of a chimneysweep, the new guard will think nothing of it when I depart. If he asks, I will explain I came in to clean the fireplace before the monk arrived. When you leave, remember walk very slow, head bowed. If someone should speak to you, just nod. Some of our brothers have taken vows of silence so your silence will not seem peculiar."

Every muscle in my body shook with fear as I listened with the utmost care to those same instructions. I repeated to myself that I could do this. Most of the guards except for Aidan never struck me as being super smart. I am smarter than most of them since I would never work for such a conceited woman. Once in charge of my feelings, I was ready to go. I watched as the monk took some soot from the fireplace and rubbed it on his face and arms. He looked at me.

"We are both set. There. Is that Pierre I see on the bridge?"

I peered out the window.

"Yes. Yes, that's him. There he goes."

"Remember my child, walk slowly. After all, I am an old man. May your journey be peaceful and bring you much deserved happiness at its end."

I pulled the hood over my face and took a deep breath. I glanced back at Brother Louis before I opened the door. He signaled for me to leave.

I walked into the hallway as slow as I could past the new guard on duty. I held onto the railing to make sure I didn't fall as I made my way down. Head down, I kept my eyes from meeting anyone else's.

I descended the stairs, making my way through the hallway and out the door that led to the bridge. I passed several guards on the palace grounds before walking onto the bridge. A palace guard approached me. What did he want? I tried not to panic while avoiding eye contact. He stopped right in front of me.

"Are you all right, sir? You appear slow and weak perhaps unable to make the walk back to the monastery without assistance? My horse is not too far from here, may I offer you a ride?"

# Chapter Nine

I shook my head and held my breath. The guard let me go through. I felt like passing out, but knew I had to keep going. Once safely near the entrance to the forest, my eyes searched for that white horse with the silver gray mane. A stately horse and rider wearing the robe of a monk appeared as if by magic out of the bushes. I did a double take.

That beautiful animal could have been a unicorn for the lack of a horn. I walked over to them and followed them back into the brush.

Aidan called out. "Quick, get on. We are out of view here. I have to take a different route than I took on my first visit to Simon's."

I got on ready to ride full saddle. Aidan kept the horse walking through the woods until we were out of eye and earshot.

"Hold on, Danielle. Chalice, take us to Simon's."

With that command, he pulled on the reins and we galloped off into the thickest part of the forest. As we rode, my mind couldn't stop wondering what the next three days held in store for us.

Aidan and I rode off leaving the view of that iconic castle in the dust. Funny, I always dreamt about visiting the castle of my ancestors since I was a young girl. I loved to look at photos of the Loire tributary passing beneath its white gray structure. I guess I always believed my visit would be under different circumstances.

I snapped out of my thoughts and grabbed onto Aidan's waist as tight as I could. I wrapped my arms around him like an octopus as we rode through the thickest part of the forest, hoping to take advantage of what daylight we had left. Branches brushed by our faces and leaves stuck to my hair. We hit a welcome patch of smooth open grass. My relief did not last long as we became immersed in trees again all too soon.

I wasn't able to talk to Aidan. We were moving too fast and the ride over fallen leaves and brush too noisy. Still, just holding him made me happy. All of a sudden, I smelled smoke. The smell seemed to come from out of nowhere. I peered around Aidan's head and saw a thatched roof cottage not far from the edge of the forest. Aidan began to slow Chalice down to a measured trot. He turned his head toward me so I could hear him speak.

"Don't worry. Chalice has ridden this route many times before. All right, my trusted steed, show us the way home."

The horse whinnied as if he understood every word. He lifted his head and whinnied once more before walking out of the forest and into a clearing that led straight to a stable next to the picturesque cottage.

A man stared out the barn window. Could that be Simon waiting for us?

As soon as the man saw us approach, he stepped out of the barn. He waved to us as Chalice came to a complete stop at the stable door. The man grabbed his reins and Aidan leaped off first before helping me down. I looked around and over at the small cottage. Its thatched roof and clinging dark green vines reminded me of an illustration from one of my favorite children's books.

The man spoke to me. "This beautiful young lady must be Danielle. She is the one who stole your heart?"

Aidan nodded. "Danielle, may I present Simon."

I curtsied not knowing what the proper greeting was. Simon smiled.

"Ah to be young again. Danielle, you are as lovely as Aidan said. I see why he is so in love with you. Please, go inside my humble home. My Marie is anxious to meet you. She has prepared lamb stew and biscuits for you both. You'll need a solid meal before your journey tomorrow. Besides, that should give me enough time to show Aidan the maps and tell him about what people and signs to look for."

I pulled my hood back over my shoulders relieved to be among friends.

Once Simon took the saddle and tack off Chalice, he led him to his stall readied with hay and water. Simon then waved at us to follow him inside the cottage. We did.

I looked around at their humble home vowing never to complain when my dishwasher didn't work. Simon and Marie were happy just to be alive and together. I realized what an important message that is for all of us. Marie helped me take off my robe and sat me down at their table. She brought over two large bowls of lamb stew and two biscuits.

"Eat hearty my dears. You'll need your strength. I'll help you on with your robes when you are ready to leave if needed."

Aidan sat down next to me with Simon next to him. The kind blacksmith pulled out a small scroll with some scribbles on it for notes.

Simon's green eyes looked directly into Aidan's. "You must listen to me carefully. Your lives will depend on what I have to say."

I choked thinking about his last comment. He opened the scroll and stretched it out on the table using teacups as weights.

"I drew you a map from here to the coast. You must follow the path exactly to the other safe houses."

Simon removed a quill pen from its holder. He drew a squiggly line on the map before pointing to an X.

"You are here. You must follow this line to the first stop by dusk tomorrow evening. It will seem like a long ride, but if you stay on course, you can do it. At each stop, you will have a contact you must locate upon your arrival. The contact is one of our men and will give you details of the next leg of your journey. Your first stop will be to a small inland village named Patrise where you will look for the baker's sign with an owl on it."

I wondered if 'one of ours' meant the underground, but didn't want to interrupt. Simon continued his instructions.

"When you reach the village, do not remove your robes. Not everyone in that village is your friend. Enter the bakery as monks and ask if the baker, Harry, can spare some stale bread and water for brothers of the cloth. Tell him Brother Simon sent you. He will understand and escort you to the back of his shop. His home is located upstairs from the bakery. His wife will feed you and provide you with a safe place to sleep. You must, however, leave before sunrise. Lucky for you, bakers get up early. He will help start you on your trek and give you your next set of directions."

I watched as Simon outlined a route through the woods and down toward the sea.

"Now the second village you will reach is called Oriane. There you will look for the Master Wheel Pub. The owner, Anthony, is also one of ours. Tell Anthony, Brother Simon made it your duty to stop there to forgive both his sins and his customers who drank too much. The good Brother implored you to go to that specific pub ignoring the rest as a special favor.

"Anthony will understand and take you into his kitchen behind the bar where you will have something to eat and a place to rest. When you reach that pub, you will still have another day's journey to the third and last stop nearest the coast. Once there, it is imperative you look for the tailor's sign with a thread and needle on it. The tailor's name is Jerome and he will look after the both of you until he guides you to your ship. You will not get much rest that night as your ship will leave at dawn the next morning.

"From Jerome's, it is mere minutes to the coast. The trade ships to England leave at five. Jerome or one of his men will escort you to the beach where you will look for a ship called The Caledonian."

"The Caledonian," Aidan repeated the name as Simon continued.

"You must make sure the ship has a black whale on its blue flag. Ask for Sir George, her captain"

Simon walked over to the cupboard and pulled out a small sack. He walked back and put it down on the table in front of Aidan.

"Here, take this. This bag is filled with silver pieces. They are to pay the captain for your voyage. The bag is small enough to fit in the pouch on one side of Chalice's saddle. Remember do not spend it or give it to anyone else. You must keep it with you at all times. That captain takes on special passengers for silver only."

I sighed. All this was too much for my tired mind to absorb, but Simon did not stop.

"Please, both of you. Never let your guard down. Always wear your robes. Guard that bag of silver. Keep it with you at each stop. That is your fare out of here. Do not have Danielle speak to anyone except to our contacts and their wives. She should act like a mute to the captain. Do both of you understand this?"

"Yes," Aidan answered. I nodded.

"Good. Since our business is finished, Marie, how about some dinner for your tired husband and seconds for your guests."

Marie obliged. I watched Aidan wolf down a second bowl of stew as if he had never tasted food before. It was so delicious and we hadn't eaten all day, I did the same. Aidan looked at Marie.

"This is like my mother used to make. Delicious."

Simon laughed at Aidan's enthusiasm. "Once you both finish eating, please follow Marie out to the barn where hopefully you will get a good night's rest. You are as safe as you can be here. I will make sure you are up early enough to get a good head start on your day, and I'll bring you some bread wrapped in sackcloth for your journey. You will need nourishment for such a hard ride. Remember to fill your water jug from our well before you leave."

Aidan thanked Simon for his help and concern. Marie got up from the table, first handing me my robe before leading us out to the barn. It was so close to the cottage, it could have been attached. I marveled at their beautiful horses as we walked by the stalls. She escorted us to a tall wooden ladder.

"You will have to climb up to the loft where you'll be hidden and safe. Try to get a good night's rest. As my Simon said, your journey will be a tough one tomorrow."

Aidan thanked her while I walked over and gave her a big hug. "Thank you for your caring and kindness. We are perfect strangers to you. I don't know what to say."

Marie wiped a tear with her apron and hugged me back. "Just be safe my dears. Stay safe and stay together."

Marie walked out of the stable leaving us alone. I looked at the ladder. It went straight up and appeared tall enough to reach the moon. All I could think about was how glad I was I had worked out before all this happened.

Aidan wanted me to go up first. He tied our robes together with some cord given to him by Simon to make our climb easier. As we ascended, I heard Marie lock the barn door. The only light, moonlight, came in through one window in the upper section of the barn.

We both reached the loft filled with soft hay. There was not much headroom so I lay down as soon as I reached the top. Aidan lay next to me his eyes filled with desire. He rolled over putting his arms around me before leaning in for a long passionate kiss.

"I never tire of your affection but we must get rest tonight. Our journey is difficult tomorrow, but first one more kiss."

I was happy to oblige. He held me until I fell asleep. Looking back, I believe he stayed awake to watch out for Alasdair's men, dozing every now and then when he thought it safe.

As the first rays of dawn burst through that window, Aidan kissed me awake. "Danielle, wake up. We must prepare to leave."

I felt so weary I didn't want to leave, but knew our lives depended on it. We climbed down the ladder just as Simon knocked on the barn door. Aidan untied our robes and we put them on. He opened the door and went over to the well for water. Simon was outside holding the loaf of bread and Chalice's reins. Chalice was already saddled.

Simon handed the bread to me as he turned the reins and the map over to Aidan who was securing the bag of silver in the saddlebag. We thanked Simon, mounted Chalice, and rode off into the forest. As I looked back at that happy little cottage, I thought I caught a glimpse of Marie waving from her front window.

We rode most of that morning. We didn't dare stop wanting to put as much time and distance between the queen's men and us. After several hours, Aidan sensed Chalice needed a break. He saw a clear brook straight ahead and slowed the horse down. Aidan got off first helping me down before walking the horse into the stream for a drink. When they finished, he came back and we sat in the tall green grass. Aidan opened the package of bread and we shared it with the pure well water from Simon's well. I remember thinking it was the most delicious bread I ever tasted.

Once we felt rested, we remounted and rode steadily until we reached the village of Patrise. Simon had marked it with a star on the map. The afternoon ride was longer than our morning one. All three of us were tired, but strove to remain diligent.

As we approached the village, I saw a sign *Village of Patrise*. I peered around from the corner of my hood. The small French village was picturesque with a pond in the center green filled with playful ducks and surrounded by blue and lavender wild flowers. The houses were all neatly painted white with dark wood trim and thatched roofs.

Aidan slowed the horse down before stopping. He turned to me speaking in a hushed tone only I could hear.

"Keep your hood up and look for the baker's sign with an owl on it. When you spot it, poke me."

As Chalice paced through the main street of the village, I looked at all the wooden signs. At last, I saw The Wise Baker with an owl painted next to the name. I poked Aidan and pointed to the sign. We rode over to the bakery and tied the horse to the hitching post directly in front of the store. After we dismounted, Aidan removed the bag from Chalice's saddlebag and placed it in his pocket.

I was so exhausted, I felt like I was still moving. Dusk moved in like a painter covering the evening sky in tones of pink and aqua blue that complemented this quaint lush green village.

Aidan put his hand over his lips to signal I should remain quiet. I was more than happy to do so not wanting to reveal our identities. As we entered the small shop, the baker had his back turned to us. He was removing the few remaining loaves out of his front window when Aidan addressed him.

"Are you the proprietor, sir? Any stale bread for some poor monks? Brother Simon said you might feed us."

The man turned and cracked a wide smile.

"Brother Simon? He is notorious for sending his starving brothers to me. Don't they have enough food at that monastery? I received a message by carrier pigeon about your mission and that you may need my help. Yes, I am the baker. Please call me Harry. Follow me into the kitchen. I have some stale bread there I save just for starving monks and hungry ducks. It will be closing time in a few minutes and I will lock up giving us some privacy."

Aidan thanked Harry. We kept our heads down as a few villagers passed by the bakery window. No one appeared surprised to see two monks inside. Harry must do this often. Startled, I jumped when the bell over Harry's door rang.

An older full figured woman dashed inside. I caught a quick glimpse of her before turning my back to her. She was well dressed in brown linen and lace and appeared more interested in us than bakery goods.

"Am I too late to buy a loaf for dinner?"

She held a monocle on a stick up to her eye. "My, who's this? More Brothers of the cloth? Again? Harry you sure have become religious in your old age. Tell me kind sirs, what is your order since there are no monasteries near us."

Harry winked at Aidan. The baker answered the busybody. "Why Clementine, they cannot answer. They took a vow of silence. The brothers are on a mission to take care of lepers in the next village. Please, don't get too close to them, as they have already assisted some before their arrival.

"I have instructed them to wash and touch nothing. I am going to donate stale bread to them so they will leave as soon as possible. They have touched nothing and I want to keep it that way. Now please hurry and choose your loaf."

We both kept our heads down. The old lady picked a loaf and handed Harry some coin. She left covering her mouth with a silk scarf while staring at us through the front window before she departed.

Once she was out of sight, the baker closed his shop, locked the front door, and let the curtains drop down over the windows. He grabbed some loaves and motioned for us to follow him. We obliged and he led us into an old kitchen.

My mind marveled at how primitive the equipment was. Every now and again, I forget what year this was. A large brick oven built into the wall, a long wooden table with a long paddle and a rolling pin comprised the baker's equipment. Next to the table, a basin stood that contained two large buckets filled with water. I saw two small loaves of bread on the table and a wheel of cheese.

Harry walked over to the corner of the oven and pulled a scroll out of the crack. The baker brushed the flour off the table before spreading out the map.

"That darn woman has too long a nose if you know what I mean. She's the town gossip. It may be just harmless curiosity, but we can never be too sure. News of your visit will spread by morning.

"The queen's guards offer to pay for information from older residents needing extra money. Forgive me. I digress from our mission at hand. Here, my children, are your directions for tomorrow. Your ride will be long and hard, but when you reach the village of Oriane, you must look for a sign that reads the Master Wheel Pub. The owner is one of us and will be of great help to you. He will instruct you on your last stop. Remember to never let down your guard."

"I would love to take you upstairs to my home and offer you more comfort, but I hope you understand why I cannot. The stairs are on the outside of the building and easily visible to the street. There are people here who do not believe in our cause and will become suspicious."

Harry sliced the loaves of bread and the wheel of cheese. "Please enjoy the fresh bread and cheese I have here for you. I filled a pitcher of spring water next to the stove for you as well. I will take Chalice to my stable to check his hooves and prepare him for his long journey tomorrow. Don't worry. He will have plenty of hay and water once I move him out of sight.

"You both will sleep in here on the floor. I keep four heavy blankets in the corner over there for such visits. When you hear me knock tomorrow morning, you will know it is four and time to leave. You will ready yourselves to depart as soon as possible so the others I spoke of will not see you here when the sun rises.

"There is a wrapped package of rolls near the oven for you to take with you on your journey. Please refill your water jug from that large bottle in the corner we use for our drink. Now try to get some rest. You both look very tired. I will leave for now, but will return at four to prepare my shop for business and see you off. Sleep in peace my children, know that we in the underground care about your safety."

Harry hugged us both before leaving us to our restless night. We took off our robes before eating the bread and cheese. The spring water quenched our parched throats. After we finished, Aidan walked over and pulled the blankets out. He spread them down on the floor like a bed and held me tight before we got down on the floor.

"This nightmare should all be over soon. Remember I love you."

I wanted to cry but didn't. "I love you too."

Aidan placed his arm around me and I kissed him. We lay down together on the thick blankets. He held me, but I couldn't fall asleep. I heard the sound of pounding hooves passing through the village at all hours and feared it was Alasdair or the queen's men. I gasped a sigh of relief for each one that passed us by. My knight motioned for me to remain silent. He heard them as well. I was so afraid they would find us, I cried to myself.

We were both awake when we heard Harry's knock at four. Morning arrived much too soon. We got up in darkness, put on our robes, refilled our water, and took the package of rolls. We went outside to see Harry standing by Chalice. Aidan put the bag of silver in the saddlebag, shook Harry's hand, and helped me to mount. As we rode off, I glanced back at the baker sweeping his front step. I turned and looked ahead at the deep dark forest hoping our next stop would be just as safe.

\* \* \* \*

After riding but a few hours, my empty stomach became uneasy bouncing up and down on the horse. I did not complain. I appreciated the peril Aidan had placed himself in so that we could stay together. We continued to ride hard and fast. I held my breath as we rode under low hanging branches and cleared brooks by jumping over large rocks. I knew Aidan was an adept horseman and kept telling myself this journey was nowhere near as terrifying as what would happen to us if the queen's guards found us. We rode for a while longer before taking a break near a quiet stream. Aidan got off the horse first and helped me down.

"Let's rest a bit. We can wash ourselves in the clear cold water of the brook. The water will refresh your spirit as well as your body. I think it safe enough here to remove our robes for just a few minutes."

After he searched the bushes, we did just that. I washed my arms, legs, and face. Aidan was right. It was so very cool and refreshing that for a brief time I forgot all about the queen and Alasdair. I wanted to jump in clothes and all, but knew we would have to leave soon. Chalice loved the coolness of the water so much he remained in the stream resting his hooves and drinking.

We walked back to where we had stopped and donned our robes. Aidan took the rolls from his bag as well as a metal cup to get a drink from our small jug. We sat down enjoying our lunch and watching our adopted horse as he munched on grass and drank from the stream.

Aidan leaned over and kissed me. "You are the bravest woman I have ever met. You'll be glad to know we are more than halfway to our next stop. We should arrive by dusk. When we enter the village, remember to look for the pub sign. Our contact there is our next link to the ship."

I remained concerned whether our journey would end safely. Aidan helped me up before he mounted our trusted stead ready to ride to our next destination. I cringed at every unfamiliar sound I heard in the forest. My mind worked overtime wondering why Alasdair's men were not hot on our trail. I knew how much that evil sorcerer needed my body for the queen's transformation and their obvious lack of presence worried me.

With every rustling noise, I imagined Alasdair's men hiding behind every bush we passed ready to ambush us and take us back to the castle. We rode until the bright sky turned to dusk. I looked out to see a small but neat village. It was busier than Patrise, but just as quaint. Petunias in different shades of pink and purple lined the main street.

"Are you ready? Look for that pub sign," Aidan said.

We passed a blacksmith, a baker, an inn, and a chemist before I saw it. I poked him and pointed to the sign, *The Master Wheel Pub*.

"I see it now."

Aidan pulled on Chalice's reins to slow him to a walk. Once at the pub, we dismounted. Aidan hitched Chalice to the post in front. I made sure my robe was on straight and my hood was down as far as it would go over my face while Aidan took out our bag of coin for safekeeping.

As we entered the pub, I could see from the corner of one eye that all the tables were full. Aidan took my arm and led me as if I were blind up to the large heavy wooden bar.

The innkeeper gave us the once over. "Not from these parts, eh?"

Aidan nodded "No. We are poor monks traveling to the coast to bless the ships. Brother Simon said the food and drink here would surpass all on our journey."

"Aye, that Brother Simon likes his food, but especially his ale. Please take a seat here at the counter. My name is Anthony. Have you traveled far?"

Aidan nodded "Yes."

"Then, you must be hungry. If our daily special suits you, I'll set aside two plates and a couple of mugs of wine…my treat. I guarantee this will be the best food on your trip."

He leaned over and whispered, "I owe Brother Simon my life. No time now to tell that story, but any friend of his is a friend of mine."

Aidan smiled. "We deeply appreciate your kindness."

"Good. Now give me a few minutes to clean up. My night barman should be here any minute. We'll go into the kitchen where we can be alone. We'll talk there."

Anthony leaned over the bar and spoke again in a hushed tone to Aidan. "Not everyone in this room is your friend, lad, but do not worry. Everyone you come in direct contact with is. Once I get you out of the bar room you will be safe. I learned of your visit from a messenger pigeon."

*Another pigeon?* I always thought they were birds that mess up the sidewalk in front of my shop. I'm so used to the computer and the internet; I was astonished at how those homing pigeons delivered the news. I kept my hood down when I heard Anthony's night bar man report for work. Anthony announced his instructions so all could hear.

"Two more needy monks. That monastery must think I am made of money. I am going to take them into the kitchen for some left over specials and water. When you can, some of the tables out here need a good cleaning. Yell if you need me."

Before we could leave, a large patron wearing a green-feathered hat and sitting at a table in the back of the room called out, "Anthony, you sure attract a lot of monks. If I didn't know better, I might guess you were up to something."

Our host laughed. "You caught me."

I gasped under my breath, but I kept my hood down.

"These two are from a monastery that makes good red wines. I promised the head monk to feed his missionaries in exchange for twenty bottles of wine a year."

The patron chuckled. "Now that's the Anthony I know. Always thinking, 'What's in it for me?'"

Anthony winked at the man but did not respond. He looked at us signaling with his head. "You two beggars follow me."

We did as he said, following him into a large old kitchen. He latched the kitchen door from behind and breathed a deep sigh of relief.

"Never can be too careful. Take a seat by that table. I leave two stools in here for unexpected guests."

I watched Anthony go to a large pot on the stove. He dished out two bowls of beef stew and put some crusty bread on the side of the plate. I was starving. I never realized how difficult it was to live on bread and water even for a day or two until now. Bet I'd lost ten pounds since we left the castle.

I could smell the beef stew before the plate hit the small work counter. The food was delicious. The stew had a hint of wine with carrots, peas, and turnips, while the simmered beef was tender and moist. I cleaned up the gravy with the bread until my plate sparkled and drank the hearty red wine to the last drop.

Aidan watched me and smiled. He was doing the exact same thing.

"This is the best beef stew I've ever eaten. Thank you."

The bar owner looked proud. "Thank you. It's my grandmother's recipe and the bread too. She made this for us when we were young and lived on the farm. When you have finished, the basin over there holds two buckets of water so that you can wash. After you do, come out the back door and we will go to a more private place where you can get some much needed rest."

Aidan led me to the sink. He poured a bucket of water over my hands so I could wash my face and arms. He followed suit. Anthony unlocked the kitchen door and went outside. We met him out the back kitchen door. I pulled my hood forward as he spoke to us.

"Follow me to my storage shed. That is where you will spend the night. Walk slowly and keep your heads down. Do not speak. Not everyone lurking about here is part of the resistance."

I remember thinking 'lurk' was the right term to describe Alasdair's movements. We followed Anthony's instructions to the letter walking from the back door of the pub and around the side of the building to a smaller stone structure. He waved for us to follow him inside.

I looked around as we did. Shelves lined the walls filled with buckets, extra tin cups, and dried vegetables. An extra pub table was stored in the corner. Anthony walked over to the table and pulled a scroll out from underneath it. He opened it up on the table.

"Here is your route for tomorrow. It's a bit tricky since it curves.

Before you see the coast, you must reach the village of Ranway. There you will meet your next contact. Midway through the forest, look for a large bent tree branch that leans across the road. Move it out of your way and follow the road as it curves west. Our brothers in arms will move it back to make sure this natural sign remains constant.

"Remember at that tree, you will make a sharp turn to the west and follow that path all the way to Ranway."

Aidan leaned down to study the map. He held his head trying to absorb the new route.

"I see what you mean. Our route will take a sudden sharp turn by this stonewall. Are the people in these woods friends or foes?"

"Friends. All friends, but they are few and far between. Now, I have bedrolls on the bottom shelf over there as well as some crackers for your journey tomorrow. You will find clean garments to wear under your robes in the bedrolls. Leave your old garments here. We will wash them for the next visitors to use. Sleep well my friends. I will care for your horse tonight and will bring him back in the morning before dawn when you have to leave."

Aidan still looked puzzled. "What sign do we seek?' I cannot tell."

"Good thing you thought to ask. I almost forgot. The next sign you need to find is the Tailor's Needle. The sign bears a picture of a thread and needle. It is barely legible on the map. I told them not to make the print so fine on the parchment. Anyway, once inside the village you will look for the town tailor, Jerome. He, like me, helps those innocents who are wrongly accused by the queen and her wizard, and will serve as your link to the English sea captain. I will leave now so you may get some rest. Your horse will be tied outside this building tomorrow at sunrise. May you reach the coast in peace, children, and your journey be successful."

Aidan walked over and shook Anthony's hand. "There is no way I can ever repay you, but I promise to help someone else needing assistance."

Anthony nodded and left us alone. Aidan closed the door behind him pulling down the long bar to lock it. He turned and walked over to kiss me.

"This is our safest stop. We are well hidden back here and can relax a bit. Let me set up the bedrolls."

He stared at me with the look of love in his eyes. "I need your love tonight. This may be our only chance to comfort each other."

Aidan opened the bedrolls on the floor placing our clean undergarments on the counter. He took off his monk's robe before helping me off with mine. We disrobed completely before lying down together. The bedrolls were so much softer than the rough blankets we had slept on previously. Their padding made me feel like I was floating on a cloud of cotton.

Aidan moved closer putting his arm around me and pulling me in toward him. He softly caressed me before kissing my neck. He moved his gentle kisses down my shoulder. My body exploded with a deep passion. I told him I wanted him to kiss every part of me. He did so. I lay there my naked body enjoying every touch and kiss before we made love.

After we finished, Aidan fell sound asleep. I slept better that night as well with Aidan's strong arm around me.

The next morning, sunlight greeted us from a small window in the back of the shed. I woke up first and kissed Aidan awake. We got up, put on the fresh garments as well as our robes, and prepared for another long journey. Aidan grabbed the bag of silver and the package of crackers.

"Ready for travel, my love?"

I nodded. The sun was peeking over the horizon as we eased open the door to the hut. Aidan checked to make sure no one was watching before we stepped outside. We saw Chalice tied to a nearby post looking as strong and beautiful as ever. We mounted Chalice and rode away as the first rays of dawn guided our way to our next stop, our guide to the coast, the ship, and our freedom.

# Chapter Ten

We rode hard and fast not wanting to stop. We realized this was our last and only chance to reach freedom and safety. After a few hours, Aidan sensed Chalice needed a drink and a brief rest. We stopped in a field near a spring to take care of his needs.

Aidan opened the small sack of crackers and went to fill our mugs with spring water. As soon as we finished our meal and Chalice seemed comfortable, we remounted and sped off again through the thickest part of the forest looking for that bent tree branch that signaled our turn. Aidan focused on the path so Chalice wouldn't misstep on all the large tree roots. I looked as hard as I could for that branch. At last, I saw it not too far along our path.

I pointed. "Look, there it is!"

Aidan slowed Chalice as we approached the tree limb. We stopped and Aidan got down and moved the branch to the side to allow us to pass. He mounted Chalice and we made the turn with ease.

Aidan was so happy, he yelled out. "We'll soon be together for the rest of our lives!"

I felt the air change. I lifted my face to smell the glorious windy sea air. We continued to ride until the village of Ranway came into view. Sea oats lined our path. Ranway appeared older than the other villages. The weathered houses gave it the appearance of a safe haven for men of the sea.

Aidan was quick to warn me. "Put your hood down as far as it will go, my love. Not everyone here is our friend. When you see the tailor's sign, poke me. My hood will be down as well."

As Chalice walked us through town, people nodded as if we were real men of the cloth. I poked Aidan. There, two cottages away, hung the tailor's sign.

We rode over to the tailor's shop. Aidan helped me down and hitched Chalice to the post out front. My love made sure my hood covered my face even more than usual if that was possible before carefully taking the bag of silver out of the saddlebag. We were tired from our journey, and I was hungry, starving. I knew I had no right to complain after everything these kind people did for us.

Aidan gave me an "Are you ready?" look. I nodded and together we slowly walked inside the tailor shop.

The tailor stood with his back to us measuring an older gentleman for a waistcoat. Even from behind, Jerome looked the part, tall, thin, dapper in his blue-gray waistcoat. From what I could see, his gray hair was as thin as his frame and he wore a monocle. I'm sure he knew we were there because the bell over his front door rang when we entered. Aidan approached him speaking in a low voice.

"Excuse me kind sir. Are you Jerome? Brother Simon mentioned that you might be so kind as to ease our journey with some bread and water."

The tailor turned and faced us. His brown eyes gleamed. "I am Jerome but your Brother Simon lied to you."

*What? How could that be?* My heart pounded so hard, I felt like it would burst out of my chest. Aidan motioned for us to wait. Jerome finished measuring the gentleman as we stood there frozen, not knowing what to do after hearing the tailor's response. As soon as the customer left, Jerome cracked a wide grin.

"Ha. Got you good. I thought monks who made wine had a good sense of humor. No bread and water for you, only the best rabbit stew in the countryside, along with fresh baked bread and some hearty homemade red wine. Come back to my home. My wife Annette awaits your visit."

If I could have breathed a deeper sigh of relief, it would have caused a sinkhole. Jerome locked the shop door, pulled down the heavy cloth shades, and closed the curtain. He waved for us to follow him out the back door. We walked through a second door so low even I had to put my head down. Once inside, we found a cozy one- room cottage much like Simon's with a big hearth. Annette was seated at the table. She was

81

middle aged with lovely features, porcelain skin, and red hair showing some gray. Her green eyes sparkled as she stood to greet us.

"Don't worry, my dears. We will keep you safe until my Jerome sends you off to your ship, but for tonight, we must only think of solid nourishment, good company, and rest."

After hugging us both, she motioned for us to sit down at their kitchen table. We felt safe enough to pull our hoods down as she brought us two bowls of steaming rabbit stew and crusty warm bread.

"Please eat. There's plenty more if you're hungry. We are not rich in coin, but we are in love. We both hope you will feel the same way when you reach our age. You are a lovely young couple."

I had never eaten rabbit before. I never thought about rabbit that way since I kept some as pets when I was young. Under normal conditions, I probably would have passed, but I was starving and didn't want to get weak. I gathered courage by taking a big swig of the wine before trying the stew. It tasted good, and I wanted to be strong enough to make it home. Aidan and I both cleaned our bowls with the bread until we could see our own reflections. Annette watched, happy to see her cooking pleased us.

"More?"

Aidan nodded. I filled up on more bread before Jerome interrupted our feast.

"When you have finished eating, I will show you the map and provide you with bed rolls back in the shop. Your horse is being tended to by one of our brothers who will return him to you before dawn. I will wake you. You must leave then to board the ship on time. Simon probably told you I would guide you to your ship but I cannot. I have customers tomorrow morning and do not want to arouse any suspicion to your mission. I will advise you of everything you need to know tonight."

Jerome unrolled the map. "You can ride only part of the way to here." He placed his finger on a spot marked with a heart.

"At that point, another of our brothers named Paul will meet you at the edge of the forest. He will be easily recognizable wearing the brown uniform of our local councilmen. Paul will take Chalice from you so that we can provide him a safe return to Simon. From there, you must walk. You might be able to see the ship and captain from there as well. You will have to approach the captain yourselves, but Paul will advise you of that."

We listened intently. Our lives hinged on the successful completion of this last leg of our journey. Aidan thanked Jerome and Annette and asked to see the bedrolls. The old tailor took us back out front to his shop and pulled them out of a trunk. He shook off the extra small bits of cloth and lay each down on the floor.

"Sleep well my friends. Your journey to safety is almost complete."

Jerome went back to his home and left us alone to our thoughts.

Aidan took my hand. "Please do not be afraid. This is the last night before we board the ship. We can only pray that we will make it safely. They will separate us once at sea because I cannot prove you to be my wife. I need to tell you how much I love you. How much I want to marry you."

He reached for my other hand. "Please, come closer."

I looked into his eyes. My body throbbed with desire as I moved closer to him. He held me in his arms before kissing my lips. I watched him take something from his pocket. It was a delicate gold lace ring with small rubies set inside the lacework. He took my hand and put the ring on my finger.

"This ring belonged to my grandmother. She told me to give it to the love of my life. Danielle you are that love. Will you marry me?"

I couldn't believe my ears. Tears of joy streamed down my cheeks as I responded. "Of course I will marry you. Aidan, I love you with all my heart."

We kissed before disrobing for sleep. Aidan loosened the ties on my bodice as I slipped out of my undergarments. He took my hand as we lay down together.

"Danielle, this may be our last night together until we reach England. I need to hold you and feel the depth of your love. That love will carry us through whatever awaits us."

Our love has grown stronger with each day. Aidan held me so gently. I could have remained in his strong arms forever. I kissed his cheek, slowly moving my kisses onto his bare chest. We made love, love that was deep, filled with desire, and sincere. We dozed off holding each other as tight as we could.

Loud knocking woke us up all too early in what seemed the middle of the night. It was Jerome.

I was exhausted. I could tell Aidan was as well. Neither of us slept well wondering what lie ahead.

"Stay strong, Danielle," he reminded me. We're almost there." With that, he stretched and yawned, rose, and put on his clothes.

I heard Chalice whinny. Aidan helped me to rise. I dressed as fast as I could, knowing we had to make perfect time today.

A male voice whispered through the door. "'Tis I, Jerome. Hurry, you must leave for the coast now before the sun rises."

Once we were both ready, Aidan opened the door a crack to be make sure we were safe. "Let us go, Danielle. We're going to our new home."

I followed him outside, hood down. Jerome held the reins while we mounted Chalice.

"Please, before you leave my keep, there's one more thing you should know. The captain's name is Sir George. We've worked with him many times before. He demands a high fee, but we know we can trust him to complete the task. Considering his payment for your passage, he'll be most happy to see two monks board his vessel."

Aidan shook the kind tailor's hand and thanked him again before we rode Chalice out of the village and onto the path that led to the coast. We took it slow so as not to call attention to ourselves.

Once on the path, Aidan quickened the pace telling me not to look back. We rode as the sun came up over a thick forest that appeared to never end. Aidan saw a small spring fed pond. We stopped for comfort and to drink some fresh water. He took Chalice in to drink and cool his hooves.

Before we left our resting place, Aidan again reminded me. "Remember keep your head down and do not speak. We do not have far to go now. The captain may know what's going on, but certainly not the crew. We don't want to throw away our chances. Keep your disguise on until you are safely on the ship and the ship has left port. Do you understand?"

I trembled. No matter how strong I believed myself to be, no matter who I'd ever faced, this tested my psyche in a way it had never been tested before. I nodded as my body trembled with fear.

Aidan kissed me before we remounted our horse to ride to the perimeter of the forest near the coast. I rode holding on tight to Aidan still wondering why we haven't been followed.

* * * *

The trees began to thin as our path approached the coast. I grew euphoric at the thought of our journey coming to an end. I peeked around Aidan's shoulder to see a stretch of wide dark sandy beach that reached as far as the eye could see.

Aidan slowed Chalice to stop on a small hill overlooking the beach to wait for Paul. He dismounted and helped me off before taking out our bag of coin to store safely in his small leather purse tucked beneath his jacket.

A man suddenly jumped out of the brush. I gasped surprised by his sudden appearance. He put his fingers over his lips to signal we should remain quiet. He approached us, smiled, and winked before speaking softly.

"You must be from Brother Simon's monastery. He inspires many monks, doesn't he? My name is Paul. Jerome sent me a message to take good care of you. I will take Chalice back to camp where he will be safe until he is returned home to Brother Simon. If you look ahead and down yonder, you can see your ship. Captain George's red hat is visible from here. Follow the narrow path down to the beach and head straight for your ship. Do not stop. Not all sailors are your friends. They work as mercenaries and are only too happy to turn you in for coin. Go in safety, my new friends."

We watched Paul take Chalice. I had become attached to that beautiful steed and was sad at the thought of losing him. I ran back and hugged our horse goodbye. He was so valiant, so loyal. Chalice nuzzled my face. He loved us as well.

Aidan took my hand and pulled me away from him just as I started to cry. We thanked Paul before he disappeared into the forest with that beautiful and brave horse.

Aidan held me.

"Danielle, it's best not to look back. Paul is taking Chalice home."

Aidan took my trembling hand and led me down the small hill until we reached the soft sand of the beach. The walk was treacherous, especially wearing a robe with a hood. All the way down, I kept my eyes glued to the path.

When we were on level ground again, I peeked out to see a long wide beach with large rough waves. If I were here under different circumstances, I would find the views magnificent and the windy sea air refreshing.

I saw at least seven sailing vessels with their tall sails blowing in the wind. They were pulled up to the shoreline waiting for either crew or cargo. I remembered Jerome said to look for the ship with a whale on its flag. I kept my head down relying on Aidan to guide me through the sand for what seemed like an eternity. He stopped short.

"There it is. There's our ship! Not too much farther now. We must remain calm and you must follow my lead. I can see the whale on the flag and the captain's red hat. The captain is standing next to the ship with his back toward us giving the crew orders. We must proceed with caution and keep our cover."

I snuck a quick peek as we approached our intended ship. I too could see the captain standing on the beach wearing his trademark large red hat. My hood slipped a bit. A funny feeling came over me.

"Aidan don't you think it strange that we haven't seen or heard from Alasdair and his army?"

"Yes, I do. It has concerned me for a while. Not wanting to alarm you, I never discussed my feelings. There are many ways to get here. Let's hope they haven't arrived before us. At this point, we have no choice but to proceed. I'm afraid we are in too deep. Please, Danielle, we are getting close to the captain, so no more talking."

I obeyed even though I knew the risks. We slowed our pace taking deliberate steps like real monks. I wanted to run to that ship anxious to leave Alasdair and that vain queen behind, but knew we had to stay with our plan. One wrong move and, if that wizard was lurking about, he'd strike us down like lightning.

As we approached the ship, Aidan spoke to me so everyone could hear. "My fellow brother, we are mere steps away from our mission."

He then called out to the captain. "Captain George, we are from the order of St. Simon seeking safe passage to England on your vessel."

Oddly, the captain remained silent. It was as if he didn't hear us. He raised his right arm slowly and waved his hand in the air. I gasped when I saw his ring. It was Alasdair's horrid serpent ring.

I screamed, "Run Aidan. It's Alasdair"

# Chapter Eleven

The captain pivoted around to reveal my innermost fear was true. "Seize these traitors for the queen," Alasdair shouted. "Seize them now."

Quickly, unhappy sailors surrounded us and bound us with rope. Alasdair approached me, pulled my hood back, and stroked my hair with his long nails.

"The only safe passage I will guarantee for your traitorous lover is to his execution. As for you, my lovely, to please the queen. Men take them both."

Another swarm of large castle guards dressed like sailors surrounded us. They took Aidan from me, walking him back to the nearest edge of the forest before lifting him onto a wooden cart carrying a cage they had hidden in the brush.

I called out to him, but he was so far away, I feared he did not hear me. "Aidan, I love you."

The cart pulled by two work-horses made its way back into the forest with Aidan secure in the cage. I wondered how Alasdair knew where to set the trap and if any of Simon's men had betrayed him. I looked back at the ship and could see the crew's bodies scattered all over the deck. Alasdair had killed the real crew and the captain.

I looked Alasdair in the eyes. "What have you done to the captain and crew?"

Alasdair grinned. "Not to worry or crease that pretty brow of yours. They won't be assisting any more traitors to the queen. I have silenced them all for good."

The wizard tilted his head back and laughed his evil laugh.

"As for you, my precious cargo, you shall ride with me."

His men took both my bound arms and marched me up the hill to the outskirts of the forest where one of the royal carriages stood.

The driver got down and opened the door for me. "Please allow me to assist you, my princess."

I was puzzled at how they could be so courteous after my escape attempt, but that narcissistic queen needed me, that is, my body. Alasdair got in the coach, sat across from me, and smiled as if he could read my mind. He was all too eager to tell me.

"I notified the queen in front of her entire court that Aidan kidnapped you. When I informed her alone of your true treacherous act, she asked me to spare no expense or manpower to find you. I told her I would do just that. You can thank me for saving your useful hide for now, but the queen wants you to watch your handsome lover die."

What? Did I hear that right? The queen wanted to watch Aidan's execution? I couldn't bear that thought. I wanted to cry, but would not give that awful man the satisfaction of thinking I cowered to his demands. Not this woman. I might be down for the count, but I'll always look for a way up or in my case a way out. Even if I had to ask the queen to pardon Aidan as a final wish for me, a request I'm sure she would deny. At this point, I had nothing to lose. As we rode to who knew where, I kept a stone face and asked no questions. I refused to give Alasdair the pleasure of seeing me wallow in fear.

The carriage ride to a mystery location seemed endless. It took us three days to reach the coast so I imagined the return to the castle would be just as long. To my surprise, the carriage came to an abrupt stop. I looked out my window to see two brick buildings with another larger structure hidden in the trees. I spotted the cart holding Aidan. I watched sadly as they released him from the cage. Even from a distance, I could tell by his demeanor that he was frightened. I'm sure he realized his life was in grave danger. Two guards escorted Aidan into a small building.

I turned my gaze to Alasdair just as he began to speak. "Prison is just the thing to humble that brazen lover of yours. You, on the other hand, are coming with me. We will rest before resuming our journey back to the castle tomorrow morning."

He called to the driver to continue up the hill to a large field stone house surrounded by leafy green trees. When the carriage came to a stop,

Alasdair reached over and grabbed my bound wrists. He held onto them so tight he nearly stopped the circulation. He stepped out of the carriage first, yanking me down the step after him.

"You, my prize, are at her majesty's summer house. One of her ladies in waiting will help you bathe and make you look your best for your arrival at the castle tomorrow. The queen must remain enamored with your looks or I shall have to carve you up and feed you to my wolves."

We walked ten paces from the carriage when a well-dressed well-coiffed young lady stepped forward to greet us. Alasdair untied my hands leaving some rope loose like a lead.

"Suzanne, take Princess Danielle to the queen's secure room for her special guests. Prepare her for a meeting with her majesty tomorrow."

Suzanne, a queen's maid-in-training, looked very young. Her long blonde curls, wide blue eyes, and perfect complexion led me to believe she was a teenager. Suzanne was nervous, especially in Alasdair's presence. I may have been one of her first duties. She was polite, curtsied before taking me by the rope and leading me inside the massive stone manor house. I kept turning around hoping to get a glimpse of Aidan, but he had already been locked up somewhere else.

Once inside, Suzanne led me up a winding white wrought iron staircase and down a long corridor of stonewalls before we entered a room at the end of the hallway. The room had the same gold gilded furniture as the castle. The walls were painted a soft green with royal blue brocade drapes. It was lovely if not for the circumstances. Suzanne walked us inside, stopped to lock the door behind us, and unbound my hands.

There was no point in fighting. I knew I couldn't escape. She dutifully helped me undress, wash, and prepare for bed. *Bed? Who could think of sleeping at a time like this?*

"My lady, while you are here, I remain your servant. I have placed a light dinner on the table before your arrival and will bring you your morning meal at dawn's first light, along with a change of clothes for your meeting with the queen. If you need anything, please pull the cord near your bed and I shall answer. Goodnight, my lady. Sleep well."

I answered politely even though I secretly wished for a crowbar, a pistol, and a fast horse.

"Goodnight, Suzanne. Thank you."

She left and locked the door behind her. There was no point in taking my frustrations out on her. She was just doing her job.

I opened the covered dish on my night table to find crusty bread and cheese, a pitcher of water, and a crystal goblet. I wondered if Alasdair poisoned my water, but knew he needed me alive at least for now. I was parched and gulped down most of the pitcher. I was not very hungry, more stressed, but I could hear Aidan telling me to eat to keep my strength, so I ate.

I couldn't sleep no matter how hard I tried. I tossed and turned most of the night. I paced around the room until the first rays of light came through my window. I soon heard a gentle knock on my door.

"My lady,' tis Suzanne, your highness. Please allow me to enter."

I responded a bit reluctant. "Please enter."

I heard the lock turn. Suzanne carried in my breakfast tray before helping me dress. I had taken my ring off last night and placed it on my nightstand. When she wasn't looking, I picked it up and put it in the skirt pocket of my new dress. I was lucky Alasdair hadn't noticed it on the carriage ride here.

Suzanne said she was under strict orders from the wizard to bind my hands loosely again. When she finished, she led me out to Alasdair who was standing by the carriage door.

He pushed me up the steps and inside. Then, he got in and called out to the driver that he was ready to leave. We left at once. By now, I had no idea where Aidan was or if he was still alive. I was beside myself with worry.

The carriage moved at such a fast pace, the morning seemed to fly. We took a different route back, a shorter one, arriving at the castle late that afternoon. Since Alasdair thought I looked presentable, he immediately took me in to see the queen.

He dragged me into the throne room. "Your Majesty, I have used all my powers to find and return the young princess. I hope that pleases you."

The queen stood and stared at me before stepping down from her throne.

"It does. Danielle, your insolence disappoints me. There will be no more favors granted. Alasdair has been instructed to make your journey to the afterlife as painful as possible. Now, let me look at you to make sure that I am not receiving damaged goods."

The queen took a monocle from her skirt pocket and held it up to her right eye to inspect my face, my hands, and even squeeze my torso.

"Where is the traitor Aidan?"

Alasdair bowed. "You'll be pleased to know he has been captured and returned in shackles to stand trial and face execution eight days hence."

"Delightful. Good work my loyal wizard. I'll be happy to reward you with our tryst once my transformation is complete."

How could she even say that to such an evil man?

Queen Katherine turned to inspect me one more time. "Danielle, I must say you still look beautiful. Amazing, considering what you've been through. Not a scratch on you. That's all the better for me. Alasdair, take her to a secure room in the dungeon. Let her see how the other half lives. I can't afford to have her escape again. I have little time left to reschedule a postponed ball."

Little time? How much is little? At this point, I thought my goose was cooked. Alasdair pulled me out of the throne room, down the hall, and out of the castle. He led me down a long outside staircase. The steps were winding and brutal. We reached the ground floor before approaching a door with a large iron gate. Two burly guards stood watch inside.

Alasdair bellowed to the guards as loudly as he could. "Guards, come now."

Two large men ran from inside toward the gate. After they opened it, Alasdair shoved me into their arms

"Here. Take this traitorous prisoner to her cell. She shall remain with the others scheduled to die. This wench is property of the queen so be gentle with her. No beating or torture of any kind. I better not see the tiniest scratch. I shall return for her in three days when she is scheduled to meet her end by my hands."

As soon as Alasdair finished speaking, the two muscular guards grabbed me ready to lead me through the gates. They stopped when they heard Alasdair issue a stern warning.

"Danielle, do not try anything tricky. I will catch and destroy you. I will not see you again until that wonderful day three days hence when we shall meet again as lovers and you shall witness my amazing wizardry and magic firsthand. What a pity, it has to be under such adverse conditions."

Alasdair walked a short distance before vanishing into thin air.

* * * *

With one large guard on either side of me, I walked down a dark hallway. It led to a damp dungeon. We passed women crying while others banged on the cells' heavy metal bars with tin cups, trying to capture our attention. We walked by at least twelve screaming women before the guards stopped in front of an empty cell. They shoved me inside with all their might. Luckily, I fell on a bale of hay in the center of the cell.

The guards followed me inside and cut the ropes that restricted my wrists. Once finished, they left, slamming the bars shut and locking the cell before walking back down the long hallway that led to the outside. I massaged my bruised wrists as I surveyed my grim surroundings.

The walls and floor were dirty. I saw a brownish red stain on the wall near the water bucket that looked like dried blood. There was no sink. Only two wooden buckets, one for water, one for convenience with no privacy, rested on the floor. If that stain was blood, my guess is the former cellmate slashed her wrists just to get out of here. I feared I would never escape. The bale of hay was my bed while the only light came from a barred window near the ceiling that would make my cell dark all day and all night.

I thought about suicide, but remembered what a wise old customer once told me. "Danielle, if anyone drives you to the point of suicide, return the favor."

I wanted to drive Alasdair to that point, hoping he would take that witch of a queen with him. Wouldn't it be wonderful to see Alasdair lose all his powers making him want to slit his magic wrists? Enough wishful thinking, I had to think of a way out.

What's that? Footsteps? Someone was approaching, but why would anyone be coming for me now? It wasn't my time. The queen would be more than willing to start the procedure early. I have to get out of here. There are so many guards and metal bars. I'm doomed. I know I'm doomed.

I listened as those heavy footsteps came closer. Cowering behind the large bale of hay, I covered my head with its straws, shuddering.

A stern male voice that reverberated down the dark prison corridor spoke. "Danielle deForet, her majesty Queen Katherine wishes to inform you your time is drawing near. That's why you are here now. Not today but very soon."

Thank goodness. Not today. He didn't come for me, but what brings the queen's grim reaper here?

I heard the guard's insidious tone. "Today, my fine damsels, Dame Rounier has the honors. Her majesty the queen orders you to prepare for your execution."

Those ominous footsteps continued to approach stopping one cell short of mine. I gasped a sigh of relief until I heard the large metal bars slide open and a woman sob.

"No, this can't be. I'm innocent. No. Please. Her majesty must believe me."

The guard laughed. "Come on, you murdering slut, you're going to meet your maker. The executioner awaits you. A large crowd gathers eager to watch you die."

"No. No. Please no. I have a young daughter." Her cries touched me.

"Good, I hope she's there to watch".

I heard him drag her from her cell. She refused to leave. She kicked and screamed all the way out until I could no longer hear her cries. The silence was deafening.

A sudden chill took my body hostage. I couldn't shake the feeling. The dungeon was damp, but my body froze from fear trembling at the thought of what they were about to do to her. I heard the crowd cheer and the swishing sound of arrows. I grew more frightened for my own safety and couldn't think straight. Crying, my thoughts darted between staying with Aidan and returning home to my mother, my life and my sweet cat, Surfer.

"Help! Someone has to help me! I have to get out of here. I'm too young to die. The queen is going to kill me. Please anyone out there, help me."

I pounded the metal bars on my dungeon cell so hard, I bruised my hands. I waited. No one answered. No one came. I had to think of how to save myself. I scanned every inch of my dreary cell desperate for a way out. Frantic, I studied the one small window protected by rusty metal bars, but already knew it was too high and too secure to do me any good. I had to face reality. There was no hope of escaping. Still my psyche refused to give up clinging to the slimmest chance that someone heard and would come to rescue me. No one knew where I was. The only man who could save me, Aidan, the love of my life, faced execution because of his feelings for me.

Exhausted, I collapsed on the dry bale of hay that served as my bed. My thoughts consumed by the hope of seeing my brave knight again, of looking into his kind eyes, and feeling the gentleness of his touch. If I could, I would risk my own life to free him, but how?

Drained by anxiety and stress, my mind drew a blank. My heart ached at the thought of never again seeing the brave young knight who stole my heart and tried to save my life. I cried, accepting the fact I was destined to die in a distant time and place by way of an evil wizard's spell.

I sobbed thinking about my mom and my cat, Surfer. I missed them so much. Wanting to feel as close to home as possible, I took the photo of Surfer I always kept with me out of my pocket and removed its plastic covering.

What's this? Another piece of paper? A card? Strange, I didn't remember putting it there. It must be from my store. Could I have carried it with me since I left?

I was curious, but for now just seeing something else from my time and home comforted me. I looked the card over with care.

It was one of Georgina's, the gypsy in my antique fortune-telling machine. To be honest, her stupid fortune telling cards angered me, but this card appeared different from the others. It was older and had a beautiful drawing of the moon, the sun, and stars on one side and a saying on the other. Why hadn't I noticed this before?

I separated the card from the photo and turned it over to read what it said. In the middle of all this absolute horror, I couldn't believe Georgina the Gypsy Fortune-Teller's card made me smile. I'm sure the machine dispensed it before my problems began. Then again, Georgina is a sore subject with me.

A dealer of rare antiques, Georgina was my antique shop's prime acquisition. I bought her about a year ago from the estate of a wealthy collector of antique amusement devices. I remember his sage advice.

"Miss Danielle deForet, congratulations, you just made a purchase that will change your career. She is worth far more than you paid and will put your store, *deForet's Finds on Fifth*, on the map for those seeking unique and one of a kind items."

Georgina wasn't cheap, but I felt I got a fair price and would be able to make a profit on her. As soon as I advertised her sale online, my inbox flooded with hundreds of inquiries about purchasing her from all over the country and the world on a daily basis.

Before any scheduled appointment, I tested Georgina. Each time, she worked like clockwork. That was amazing considering her parts were over a hundred and thirty years old. The large white light bulbs around her cabinet lit up and rotated while Georgina, a very beautiful mannequin, squawked a bit less irritating than a parrot, "Georgina never lies."

I should qualify that. She worked for me alone until a client showed up with a twelve thousand dollar check in hand. Collectors traveled long distances to Naples Florida to see her. Of course, they asked I demonstrate if and how this antique machine worked. I obliged by putting my penny in the wooden and brass coin chute and pushing. Her delicate wooden hand with an ornate red stone ring was supposed to pass over a deck of mystical cards selecting one for her client and dropping it down the slot.

That happened for me, but throw someone new in the mix and her lights went ballistic rotating around the machine like it was ready to blast into space. The mannequin's hand shook like a cocktail mixer fumbling the deck scattering the cards all over the inside of the machine.

Ridiculous as it might seem, I began to believe she could sense a buyer. Eventually, one card would manage to drop down the slot as if by accident. As soon as the buyer left, I would try another penny and she worked like a charm. It was as if she didn't want to leave my shop. Anyway, the last time she had a mechanical tantrum, she drew a card after the customer left.

*"Your true love awaits you in a most unlikely place and time. Always remember, Georgina never lies."*

I didn't think I wanted to find true love again after I lost Josh, (my former boyfriend.) I threw the card on the floor disgusted by her entire charade. That unruly mannequin had the audacity to dispense another one. That card must be the one I picked up, placed in my pocket, and forgot about.

The peculiar thing about all this is that I did find true love in a very unusual place, a French castle, and time, 1559. I decided to read her card. At this point, what did I have to lose?

*"You will encounter grave danger. Do not be afraid. Call out to me by name. Ask me to rescue you and I will come. Remember, Georgina never lies."*

My jaw dropped. How could she possibly know I would be in danger? How could she save me from that wizard's spell? Was this a quirky coincidence or were her fortune-telling skills real? What were the odds that two cards drawn at random could predict my future? Maybe they were just the luck of the draw. Since I'm already doomed, what harm would it do to play along?"

I held her card in the air and yelled at the top of my lungs. "Georgina, rescue me."

I looked around. Nothing had changed. I wasn't surprised.

Still standing in this dreary place, I called out to her again. "Georgina, rescue me."

Still nothing. Truthfully, I didn't expect anything unusual to happen. I knew I was clutching at straws. Frustrated and despondent, I cried, sad for both Aidan and myself. I stopped when I felt something odd touch my shoulder.

I placed my hand there only to feel a cold hard hand. Startled, I turned and stared in total disbelief at who was standing in front of me. This must be from stress or lack of sleep, but how I could I feel her touch?

I blinked. She was still there beautiful as ever with alabaster painted skin and long black hair in curls tied back with a lace kerchief. Her round dark brown eyes gave me the most gentle and comforting gaze. She was wearing the same red satin dress and ecru lace shawl she wore in the machine and sported a stiff smile that showed off her permanent blush. I was not imagining things; my life- sized doll had just come to life.

I pinched myself. Georgina touched me again to let me know she was real before holding out her hand.

"Please Danielle, touch me. I am as real as you are."

I did, surprised she didn't go away. I looked into her soft eyes.

"Am I dreaming, perhaps hallucinating? How can you be real? You're a wooden mannequin in a machine."

Her response surprised me.

"I may have spent part of my life as wood, but trust me, I am no mannequin. Beneath this stiff facade lies a warm-blooded caring woman much like you. Since you called for me to help get you out of here, please do not ask any more questions. I will explain when we have more time. You and I share a great deal in common, but for now, please just do as I say."

I had to be dreaming. This made no sense.

I agreed, eager to leave. Georgina took a small whistle out of her skirt pocket.

"Come stand with me. Please close your eyes until I have finished my call, hold your arms out straight, and grab on tight to one of my hands."

I did as she said. When I heard the high-pitched whistle, I panicked at the thought of what might happen next. "Won't the guards hear us?"

"Do not worry. Only those who need to hear, will."

She whispered, "Ceresin, come to me my gentle wind. Hear my call. Ceresin, please come take Danielle forward to her time and home."

She paused. "Danielle, open your eyes."

I watched speechless as a pure white formless mist slithered into the dungeon through the inside prison gate. The mist made its way down the long dreary corridor before wrapping its mist around my cell's bars.

Georgina looked at me. Fear overtook me. Tears streamed down my face. My body shook. My arms fell limp. The kind gypsy squeezed my listless hand.

"Danielle, don't be afraid. Take my hand. Hold it as tight as you can. Ceresin will carry us home in a soft cloud of air."

Still speechless, I did as she said clutching her hard hand so tight mine ached.

Ceresin rushed into my cell. The wind poured through the bars on my door before circling the small space like a cyclone. Showing us her true force, she rushed through the bars on my cell's window, bending them back in the process. Ceresin slowed down wrapping herself around our bodies like a giant python. I felt her soft tropical air waft through my hair. Her breeze comforted me reminding me of home.

As her breeze stroked my head, Georgina smiled hoping to abate my fear. With one sudden burst, Ceresin tightened her grasp pulling us up into her form. Before I knew it, the wind lifted us off the ground. With one more strong blast, she carried us through the bent metal bars.

We flew out the window over the palace gardens and moat. I was afraid to look down but managed a peek. I screamed when I realized how high we were, but as I did, Ceresin took us higher into the atmosphere. Oddly enough, the higher we rose, the safer I felt.

Ceridian's wind was as soft and gentle as a down comforter. We floated swaying free like hawks. I looked down at the castle now a miniature; her guards tiny stick people. We spun around and around until they were no longer in sight. We drifted for quite a while before making a slow descent. I grew dizzy and blacked out unaware of what happened next.

When I awoke, I lay on the floor of my shop. Georgina waved a lace fan over me while Surfer, my cat, licked my face.

"Danielle, wake up. You're safe now. I never trusted that old sorcerer Alasdair as far as I could throw him. I need to know what he did to you. You must tell me everything from the beginning so I can plan our revenge and break the spell he cast on me as well as the one he put on you."

It took me a few seconds to catch my breath. What spell? How does she know Alasdair? Just the mention of that evil wizard's name made me hyperventilate.

Georgina patted my hand. "Take it easy, Danielle, you're safe now. I'm sorry I had to subject you to all that. Take deep breaths. Breath in then out slowly."

I shook my head in disbelief. Subject me to what? What is she trying to tell me?

"Don't tell me to breathe easy until you explain why you're sorry."

"That's a bit difficult right now. It's a long story. Very long."

I still felt out of breath. I had to calm myself down. I picked up Surfer and hugged her just as Georgina reached for my hand to help me rise.

"Please, sit down here on this bench. Take as much time as you need to compose yourself."

Georgina walked me to an antique silk brocade settee situated between my counter and her cabinet. Surfer followed only too happy to jump on my lap. She pounced from one of my legs to the other rubbing her head under my chin. I held her as tight as I could. Georgina watched our happy reunion.

"I'm so glad I heard your call. I knew where you were but because of the spell Alasdair cast on me, I had to wait to hear from you. You realize you've been gone ten days. I made sure I took good care of Surfer. After all, I was aware you Traveled with that dangerous stranger."

Aware? She was aware and did nothing to help?

"You mean to tell me you knew where I was and who I was with and you did nothing to rescue me after all I've been through with your tricks in my store."

Georgina hesitated. "Well, I don't know every little detail of your Travel. Besides, I needed you to call me to partially break my spell before I could assist you. You do remember I could speak only three words. Now fill me in so I can cast a spell on him for both of us."

I was stunned. "You cast a spell? You don't even work with a penny. You know how incorrigible and evil that man is. You must have meant you wanted to help me rescue my love Aidan. I'd prefer not see Alasdair again, if I can help it."

Georgina sat silent, quite a feat for her now that she could say more than three words.

"Are you sure we're far enough away so that evil wizard can't find me?

Georgina nodded. I looked at her still shocked to see her standing before me.

"I must have fallen and bumped my head on the floor. This whole episode is a bad dream. You're just a contusion."

The gypsy reached for my hand. "I'm afraid not. I'm as real as you are. I warned you danger was in the cards for you. Why didn't you listen to my warning?"

"Would you listen to a hundred-and-thirty-year old fortune telling machine that malfunctioned more than it worked? You don't exactly invoke confidence."

"Just remember, young lady, that if I had worked and you had sold me, I would not have been here to protect you. Your rescue is worth more than a measly twelve thousand dollars." She knew I had no answer for that. "Besides, you were gone for ten days before you had the good sense to call me. I was thrilled to hear your call. I recognized that old goat's voice and knew he was up to no good the minute he came into our shop."

"Our shop? That old goat? How did you know him?"

"I have grown to love our shop and think of you as family. Sadly, there are so few of us true wizards good or bad left. I had a run in with that old goat a few years before he held you captive. We share more in common than you think."

I closed my eyes hoping everything would disappear from my memory except Aidan. When I opened them again, everything remained the same.

"Ten days? That's all? It felt like an eternity especially if you knew what happened. You know I didn't go willingly. That man kidnapped me."

My emotions got the better of me. Tears streamed down my cheeks. I managed to pull myself together.

Georgina squeezed my hand.

"That wizard and I go way back. Hundreds of years to be precise. You Traveled to the castle only a few years after he cast a spell on me. Now that some of my powers have returned, I intend to seek revenge for what he did to us. At first, I believed you did not call because you didn't want to see me anymore especially since no one wanted to purchase me. I thought you might have given up on finding true love. I knew I was wrong when I heard your precious call for help—"

"Precious? Desperate was more like it. I can never thank you enough. You saved my life, and you were right. I did find love in an unusual place and time. Aidan's my real knight in shining armor just like those handsome men on the covers of romance novels."

"Ah, like the ones you keep under the counter. Tell me all about your Aidan. Who is he and where did you meet him?"

I sighed.

"My love story borders on the bizarre; like a fairy tale with an evil sorcerer, a wicked witch of a queen, and a handsome knight, but believe me, it's all true. I know I put myself in peril because I was greedy, but I fell head over heels in love because of my mistake. I need your help. If you truly have the special skills of which you speak, Georgina, I need your magic to work now. I'll promise never to sell you, no matter how large the offer price. I have to save Aidan from execution."

My eyes pleaded with Georgina. Her eyes left my face and focused on the ornate gold dragon broach with ruby eyes on my dress.

"That's a lovely pin. It's from sixteenth century France, is it not? Diamonds, rubies, fit for a queen."

"It belongs to Queen Katherine. I could care less about it, but I do care that you heard that man take me and did nothing to stop it."

Georgina waved her stiff finger at me. "I was under his spell and could not speak more than three words. I gave you my card, but you failed to heed its warning. You didn't believe."

"How could I? You were a malfunctioning mannequin. At any rate, that nasty man kidnapped me and took me back to 1559 and Chenonceau Castle in The Loire Valley of France."

Georgina nodded, "Ah. Chenonceau. One of the most beautiful castles in the world. Surrounded by water, it boasts a tower that houses a poison room any wizard would envy and delight any royal with murder on his mind. It served the crown as an apothecary, but, believe me, many deadly potions were mixed there."

"That's quite enough. I didn't go there for a tour. I was kidnapped to be murdered. Please, tell me how you plan to rescue Aidan."

Georgina remained calm despite my total insolence and disrespect. My last answer made her react like an angry Rhodesian ridgeback.

I continued to taunt her hoping to find out the truth. "You must know I had no intention of time traveling. I repeat. I was kidnapped."

The gypsy scowled. "Go on, tell me the entire story."

I swallowed hard still reeling from my rescue. I then recited my encounter with Alasdair and the kidnapping.

"Nice to know I'm appreciated. Next time, in case I am not around, remember safety first. You shouldn't talk to unusual strangers no matter how much money is involved. I'm quite sure your mother already told you that. I am not upset. After all, when you called me, you broke one of the spells which made it possible for me to help you."

I sighed. "Mom always gave me good advice, but that doesn't help my poor Aidan right now. How will we rescue him?"

Georgina smiled. "We? I rescued you. I don't recall giving Aidan a card. Besides, you're the one who left me high and dry once you took off with that wizard making me wonder if I would ever be free of this wooden box. Your abrupt departure could have hurt me, if I had not been using you as bait to draw Alasdair to me to break his spell."

"Break his spell? I was kidnapped by an evil wizard and was about to die. I'm beside myself with fear. Please don't refer to me as bait."

Georgina stared at me. "We all do things in life that are necessary for survival. I'm sure you have. Now, I'll grant you fell in love along the way, but you still have to tell me why I should help Aidan?"

"Georgina, you're the one who gave me that card. Remember? You will find true love or whatever it was. Well, I did and he's it so since this is your fault. All of it. You have to help. I love him. He risked his life to save me. How would either of us know we were bait? He will be executed in six days if I don't go back and help him."

Georgina looked pensive. "Where do you plan on taking him after his rescue?"

"Why here with me."

"Interesting for a woman with no powers, only baggage."

Her eyes lit up like a neon sign. "Come to think of it, Aidan's presence may be just the trick I need to draw that unscrupulous Alasdair here. That nasty old goat has to come to me of his own volition. Then and only then, can I overcome the power of his magic and release the three of us from his evil spells."

Georgina paced back and forth stopping in front of her wooden cabinet. "Tell me, Danielle, where do you think he is now?"

"I don't know. I think he's probably rotting in a dirty prison cell with a view of the prison yard. Please help. He'll be executed if you don't."

Georgina listened to my deepest fears before speaking. "I have a strong feeling that may not be the case. Maybe we should look in on him."

She reached deep into her skirt pocket and pulled out a deck of cards. She shuffled the deck.

"Danielle, as you have learned, these cards are not for amusement. These are special, belonging to my grandmother, and having great powers over someone's destiny. For my magic to work, you must draw seven cards. I can see by the look on your face you wonder why seven. In ancient Chinese cultures, the symbol for seven represents togetherness. It is a lucky number for relationships. Since we want to get yours back together, I need all the help you can give me."

The gypsy walked over to the counter, placing the shuffled deck face down. She fanned the cards out before closing her eyes.

"Great cards of life, love and happiness," she whispered, "use your most powerful magic to help guide Danielle on the path of true love."

I stood skeptical of this whole magic bit, but I couldn't believe my eyes when the lights on her cabinet erupted in all the colors of the rainbow swirling around the frame so fast they made me dizzy. Georgina glanced over indicating I should be serious.

"Since you are the one in love, please select seven cards from the deck. Do not look at them, just place them face down next to the deck over here."

She pointed to a place not too far from the main deck. I walked over and looked at her special cards. They were not the cards I had seen her dispense hundreds of times before from her machine. These were very different with artwork on the back that looked very old. Come to think of it, the card I found in my pocket was from this deck. If they possessed true magic, my future with Aidan rested in their hands. I took a deep breath and drew seven cards. I closed my eyes as tight as I could and placed the cards down where Georgina had indicated.

Just like that, those shooting balls of light that outlined her machine came on again swirling around the store. A kaleidoscope of color filled the room. Rose, purple, blue, and pink lights circled the walls mesmerizing me as I watched.

The streams of color raced around the room like comets. Their motions began to slow down to soft pulsating movements like those of a beating heart. I had just poured my heart out to Georgina about my adventure. I told her that Aidan was the one –the love of my life. Before I had been kidnapped, I always avoided any kind of date, not wanting to get involved. I think she was intuitive enough to sense how lonely I was before I met Aidan. I never talked about why. My heart was too broken to tell anyone about it. I didn't want questions or pity from well-intentioned matchmakers.

Not since I lost the love of my life, my fiancé Josh, in Afghanistan three years ago, had my heart been willing to open up to love. My friends tried to introduce me to guys, but none could ever hold a candle to Josh. He was so strong, so brave risking his life for his country by serving in the Marines. He was proud to wear his uniform and proud to serve. I still miss him more than anyone can imagine. I thought true love would never come for me again, but now it has in a most unusual way. I guess strong men in uniform always hold a special place in my heart. Aidan could never replace Josh or my love for him, but I fell in love with Aidan in a different way.

My mind snapped back to the present. I looked at Georgina. She remained intent on reading the cards. All of a sudden, the colored lights stopped rotating. Georgina leaned in as if she had something very important to tell me.

"Danielle. I will now read your cards. Do you have any questions for them?"

I nodded. "Is Aidan still alive?"

Georgina turned the first card over. She read aloud. "Your true love withstands the test of time. That is a yes."

I took a deep breath and watched as she slowly turned over the rest of the cards. A worried look came over her brow.

"The remaining cards act as a guide to show me what happened. It seems we have complications, my sweet."

"Complications? What kind?"

Georgina turned, removed the crystal ball from her cabinet, and set it on the counter next to the cards.

"This is my grandmother's crystal ball. Its accurate predictions are legendary. When Alasdair placed me under his spell, I had the forethought to change his glass ball in the cabinet to my own using mental telepathy. I am glad we now have its powers to help Aidan."

The gypsy closed her eyes and waved her hands over the crystal ball whispering words I couldn't understand. The ball lit up. Rose- colored smoke swirled inside of it. Georgina kept her gaze on the ball until the smoke cleared.

"There. I can see where Alasdair has paid our young knight a visit in jail. I can hear that nasty wizard lie, telling Aidan that you escaped again and may not be on your own. He further inferred that some witnesses saw you leave with the queen's favorite footman, Thomas, the handsome one. Aidan was beside himself with anguish thinking you betrayed his love. He wondered why you would do such a thing if you still loved him. Alasdair laughed, telling him, having no love and no friends now makes his only friend the executioner. Aidan put his head down in his hands looking totally distraught. He must really love you."

I became frantic as I watched her stare into the ball. She watched for what seemed like forever. I broke her concentration.

"Of course he loves me. How many times do I have to tell you that? He risked his life for me. I have to get to him and tell him the truth about me."

Georgina shot me a look of disappointment. "Which truth? About Thomas or that you were a Traveler? You never revealed to him that you Traveled from a different time or did you just omit that fact from your qualifications to be temporary queen?"

She knew how to make me feel guilty. "I didn't hide that fact to hurt him. If my body got transformed, I would have been turned to dust. I breezed through the facts once when we first met, but he seemed puzzled and unwilling to believe me so I dropped the subject. I never brought it up again since the right opportunity never presented itself again. What should I do now?"

"At the first appropriate moment, you must tell him. As for now, we don't have much time. The first thing you will do is go to your office and shower and change your clothes. I know you keep extra clothes in there. Wear dark pants and a dark shirt that will help hide you. After you dress, come out to me. Please do as I say. When I reveal the last card, you will learn there's much more to this story."

Her last remark angered me. "More? How dare you hold anything back from me?"

Georgina touched my hand. "Calm down. The rest of this message may be good for both of us. Let me turn the last card over now to ease your concern."

She turned over the last card. It was a king. The eye in his profile stared right into my eyes.

The gypsy looked at me and smiled. "The king is the best card we could hope for. It symbolizes Aidan's strength and perseverance to escape Alasdair and find you. I will look in my crystal ball to see whether he did."

Georgina bent over the lavender colored ball. Her eyes opened wide. "What a nice surprise. Once the wizard left Aidan's prison cell, Simon and his small band of resistors whistled a recognizable sound outside his window."

I remained puzzled. "What good is that? There are guards out there at all times. Only one guard has the ring of keys to the cells. That guard could kill Simon with just one swing of his sword if he tried to take the keys away."

Georgina shook her head. "Not if Simon had one of his friends drop a heavy rock on the guard's head from the tree adjacent to the prison wall. A friend of Simon's, a man carrying two large rocks in a net and dressed in forest green, climbed the tree before dawn and stayed as still as a statue waiting for Alasdair to leave. There is only one guard on duty midday so the other guards could take their lunch. The green man, being a trained hunter, remained patient and quiet, before striking his prey on the head with the rocks he carried.

"The man in green whistled for Simon who brought rope to scale the wall. Once on the ground inside, Simon removed the keys from the unconscious guard's belt and whistled for Aidan. Aidan recognized the familiar call of the woodsman and whistled back. Simon raced to Aidan's cell and freed your knight."

"They left the area as fast as they could. Simon did not want Aidan or any of his men near the courtyard when the guard recovered. They rode back to Simon's cottage. Aidan remains there now. That's very close to where I will be sending you. Now that you have heard the entire story, please hurry and ready yourself."

I didn't stop to ask any more questions. I was too anxious to see my love. I raced into my private office bathroom. Surfer followed jumping on the sleep couch.

I looked around. Georgina had everything ready for me. She knew exactly what I needed. She had placed the softest towels and lavender scented shower gel on my desk. I undressed and placed the ruby ring from my pocket in my desk drawer before getting into the shower. As the hot water ran over my tired body, the fragrant lavender soap brought back memories of that beautiful but dangerous part of the French forest and our trek through the woods.

I dried myself with the towel and dressed before combing my hair and tying it back. Once ready, I put a fountain pen in my pocket and gave Surfer a big hug and kiss before returning to the store.

Georgina stood at the counter studying those same cards. The odd smile on her face concerned me. I walked over to her.

"Any more news?"

"Not exactly. Just gloating over how many of my skills have returned. I need to see how and when Alasdair discovered you missing. It will give me a picture of his mindset. We are dealing with a monster, you know."

"I know but how can we see his reaction?"

Georgina looked into her crystal ball once more. "Aren't crystal balls magnificent? Today's wizards and seers do not rely on them as much as we did in our day. Please stand directly behind me. Place both of your hands on my shoulders. Touch is very important."

"I learned that the hard way."

"Yes, you did from Alasdair. Look straight ahead. I will make the scene appear over the crystal ball and in the air. You will be able to see and hear everything. Be quiet and stand very still."

Just the fact that Georgina was so concerned, I was sure Alasdair was using every available resource to find Aidan. I wanted to believe the love of my life was safe. I would risk everything to reach him before it was too late.

## Chapter Twelve

As soon as I touched Georgina, a cloud of soft light appeared over the crystal ball. Forms began to take shape in the cloud. I could see Alasdair. At that moment, he was unaware of any escape. He was busy mixing the potions for the queen's transformation.

Katherine required Stephanie take care of my meals while I was in the dungeon. The queen did not want the dungeon's horrible menu to ruin my skin or make my body have offensive odors. Stephanie was on her way to my cell to bring me breakfast and tea along with a change of clothes for a meeting with the queen. A royal guard escorted the young maid, afraid to walk by all the screaming prisoners alone.

She gasped when she looked through the bars and did not see me. She ordered the guard to unlock the door at once. Stephanie dropped the tray and dress and ran inside to see if I was all right. She ordered the guard to move the bale of hay to make sure I wasn't sick, passed out, or had fallen. She looked up at the window. It remained closed. Stephanie knew the cell door could only be opened with a key.

She demanded the guard ask the men at the gate if they had seen anyone leave. He returned soon to report that no one had seen or heard anything.

"How shall I ever break the bad news to Alasdair?" Stephanie muttered. "He will have to face his worst nightmare with the queen. What shall become of me?"

I watched Stephanie sob. She was beside herself realizing that she had to be the one to tell that nasty wizard. Stephanie had always been kind and loyal to me and should not take the blame for my actions especially with Alasdair. She stopped for a moment and decided to let out a blood-curdling scream for help.

It echoed throughout the castle. By now, the wizard, who was on his way to my cell to escort me to our meeting with the queen, heard her scream for help. His walk turned into a run as he raced down the dark hallway to find Stephanie alone in my cell, sobbing on the bale of hay. Tears streamed down her face as she looked up at him.

"My most powerful wizard, I found her cell empty. I searched every corner to make sure she wasn't hiding or hurt. Please forgive me. The window was sealed shut and the door locked."

I smiled as I watched that nasty man pound his fist on the bars as he listened to Stephanie report every detail. She got down on her knees and begged his forgiveness again. Alasdair ordered her to stand.

"Stephanie, you are her majesty's most trusted maid. How could you have known about this when even a masterful sorcerer such as I had no idea? I believe you, now you must do me a favor. We must find Princess Danielle for the queen. Word of her escape will only impede events. You must swear to me that this shall remain our secret. It is in the queen's best interest to do so. Tell me. Swear on your life that you will do this for me."

Stephanie looked fearful. Tears still streamed down her face, but she remained silent. Alasdair tried to convince her that she was doing the right thing by listening to him. Her loyalty to the queen impeded her decision.

Despite his obvious anger, he struggled to convince her. "Stephanie, I am sure you did not want this to happen. You alone know how important Danielle is to her majesty. Now I must ask you again to swear on your life that this will remain just between us. You must not worry the queen. Do you understand?"

Stephanie looked up in total fear of Alasdair. Trembling, she nodded.

"Yes, I understand. I will not say anything about this to anyone. I swear on my life."

I watched as Alasdair smiled. I knew first-hand how he enjoyed controlling people. He waved his hand to dismiss her.

"Wipe your tears before serving your queen. You cannot cast any aspersions. If she asks about the meeting, tell her I left the castle for a brief time to seek more herbs and haven't as yet returned."

Stephanie wiped her eyes with her lace handkerchief, curtsied, and left.

Alasdair's eyes turned fire engine red. "How dare that wench think she can outsmart me? I'll show her the full force of my power. She will be sorry. If only I did not need her body for the queen, I would dissect her piece by piece and feed her to my wolves."

Georgina interrupted our watch. "Pure evil flows through that man's veins. Feed you to the wolves. Awful thought. Just awful."

We watched, as Alasdair demanded the guard posted at my cell call for his two most trusted men. They arrived and the wizard called them into a huddle.

He spoke in a low voice but we could hear every word thanks to Georgina's crystal ball. "This task I am about to assign to you must be done with the utmost secrecy. No one must know about our problem. You will speak only to me about this. Princess Danielle has escaped from the dungeon. We do not want the queen to worry. That insolent young woman could not have gone far on foot. I need you to search every inch of this castle and its grounds. Now hurry."

The guards raced off, not wanting to disappoint the wizard. Alasdair remained in my cell looking for any clues I may have left behind, but there were none. Everything I owned was in my skirt pocket and Traveled home with me. He'd have to be smarter than a crime scene investigator to find any evidence of my whereabouts.

Alasdair remained in my cell a long time. He threw the buckets against the wall, aggravated at his failure to find anything. He muttered he better send a guard to check on Aidan before leaving to return to his potion room.

The two guards sent to search the grounds approached Alasdair as he walked to the castle.

"Well, what did you find?" Alasdair demanded impatiently. "Did you find her or any clue as to where she went?"

The guards hesitated to answer. One spoke.

"We searched all over the grounds and rode into the village. No one has seen her. It is as if she vanished into thin air."

Alasdair dismissed both of them. "You may go but keep your eyes and ears open. She cannot be far away. She does not have a horse. Remember, our quest must remain a secret. We would not want to incur the queen's wrath. If you need me, I will be in my potion room. If you discover anything, come to me at once. Now go check on the traitor Aidan."

I watched him climb the stairs to his room of potions and poisons muttering all the way.

"There's more to Danielle then meets the eye. Beautiful but crafty. I like my women to be smart and have a little spunk, but now I wonder if she has a secret sorcerer. If so, who could that be? It's difficult to find a more talented sorcerer than myself. I knew of only one and I fell in love with her. I cast a spell on her so that rules out Georgina. Yes, another sorcerer is the only plausible answer to her clean escape. I must get to the bottom of this and soon before the queen finds out Danielle is missing and I will be out of her good graces. That ungrateful old woman can be just that fickle."

Alasdair entered his room of poisons and began to go to work. One of his guards ran in frantic to get the wizard's attention.

"Alasdair, sir, please come now. The traitor Aidan has escaped from his prison cell as well. He is nowhere in the area. Someone knocked out the guard carrying the keys to his cell with a large rock. We found the keys on the ground near the prison wall. Please, we need your wisdom and instruction as to how to proceed."

I looked down at Georgina and laughed. "Nice to see Alasdair is having a bad day."

"It is, but for now we must find your lover."

I watched the vision as that dreaded smoke seeped out of Alasdair's nostrils. He was so angry he pounded his fists on the counter. He could not believe his ears.

"Both prisoners gone? How could that be? What kind of fools do I have under my command? Take me to his cell now! I need to see this for myself."

The guard escorted Alasdair to the prison yard and into the dungeon to look at Aidan's cell. The wizard rushed back out to the courtyard and called all of his guards together.

"Men. Come close. Aidan and the princess have escaped. We are not dealing with average prisoners and need not alert the queen. I need six of you with strength and wit to comb the forests outside the village. I know there are bands of rebels there assisting political prisoners. I'm sure our two friends are aware of them as well. Someone must be protecting them. That person may be a commoner or a sorcerer. Use whatever force is necessary to make those traitorous rebels talk. The two prisoners have to be nearby. Now let me see some volunteers."

All the guards raised their respective hands not wanting to offend the powerful wizard. The wizard walked by each of them selecting six men with care.

"All right then. Marcelle, Stalle, Christophe, Herman, Brendan, and George, you are the chosen six. Prepare yourselves. Bring your most vicious weapons. If either of those two traitors resist, kill the knight, but bring the woman back alive. Take handcuffs and other physical restraints with you. We must find them for our queen. Now go. If you need to search outside the village, you may ride to the middle of the forest but will have to walk from there to the deepest part."

The other guards, looking formidable in their black knit uniforms bearing the wizard's dragon crest, raised their swords as a measure of solidarity even though they were secretly relieved they were to remain in the castle.

Alasdair flashed his red eyes over those remaining guards. "I repeat. No one must learn of the prisoners' escape. If I find out that one word of their escape left this group, I can assure you personally that any one of you may wake up with two heads or no feet. Understand? You all will give me your word bound by your lives."

They raised their hands to repeat Alasdair's pledge. "I pledge on my honor as a member of Alasdair's guard that I will not reveal any news regarding the prisoners' escape to anyone except my group of fellow brothers of the sword."

Alasdair nodded. "Remember, I will be watching each of you. Those not in the search party are dismissed. You six will return with me to the traitor's cell. I want to make sure we did not overlook any clues as to his intended direction."

The six guards led the furious wizard to Aidan's cell. Walking inside, Alasdair studied every inch and followed Aidan's trail outside to the wall.

"How careless of that insolent guard with the keys. If that lazy man did not take a break under the tree, Aidan would still be here awaiting his appointment with death. I will deal with that guard personally. The six of you have my complete trust. I know that you are the best of the best."

Georgina and I watched as the six guards formed a straight line facing that nasty sorcerer who paced back and forth in front of them.

"You are my best men. Go fetch that woman and make her lover pay for his errant ways. Make that insolent royal know I am still in charge of her fate. Do not make their arrest easy. Now, off you go. Time wastes. May your journey bring success for our queen. Remember Princess Danielle must come back unscathed, but frightened out of her pretty mind."

Alasdair's eyes flared red as he addressed the guards again. "If you fail, you understand the mistake will cost you your lives. Now leave."

I looked at Georgina.

She motioned for me to be quiet and pay attention. I looked into her crystal ball again.

The six guards marched out of the cell and the prison yard as a unit. They mounted their horses and rode toward the village. Halfway there, they stopped by a stream for a drink.

Marcelle, the most experienced guard, called the group together. "We need to name a team leader, someone able to take charge of our actions."

The others remained silent.

One voiced his opinion. "I vote for Marcelle. He has been on more manhunts than all of us put together."

The men lifted their swords in a show of solidarity. Marcelle thanked them for their trust before leading them into the village.

With a stern face, he addressed them. "If those two traitors left our castle grounds, they had to leave on horseback. Once they arrived in the village, their horse or horses would need tending. That's why we will start our search in the stables of the village. Find any stable hands, grooms or horse owners, anyone who has anything to do with horses. Stop and question them. Make them shake with fear. Squeeze information out of them. That's the only way we will find out where those two went. Remember Alasdair said it is us or them."

The six guards mounted their horses and rode into the village. They dismounted when they reached the village square, hitching their horses to the public posts. Marcelle spotted a nearby stable. He told his men he would search that one while they scattered to locate and search all the other stables in the village.

Once his guards left, Marcelle entered the nearby stable looking for any leads. He poked around the stalls seeing only the horses.

Marcelle muttered to himself, "Wish horses could talk."

He continued to poke around all of the nooks and crannies of the main area until he spotted a small parchment document rolled up and tied under some hay near the front door. He picked it up, opened it, and spread it out with care on the long worktable in the center of the stable. His eyes lit up when he saw it was a small map of the surrounding forest. The map displayed the thickest part of the forest. He ran his finger over a line to the center of the forest when he noticed an 'X'. It marked a small cottage.

Marcelle removed a monocle from his pocket and examined the document closer. "Interesting. I may have just found one of the resistors' secret locations."

Just as he finished that thought, a teen-aged boy wearing a stable uniform entered carrying a bucket of water. Marcelle dashed behind a post waiting to surprise him. The muscular young man walked over to a black horse and filled his water trough. Just as he turned to leave, Marcelle jumped in front of him blocking his path.

The startled boy jolted back dropping the bucket and spilling whatever water was left on the ground.

"Please sir, don't hurt me. I have naught for you to steal. Let me tend to the horses. They need water. It's their time to drink."

Marcelle placed his hand on his sword and frowned at the boy. "Sir Marcelle to you. I am a knight in Queen Katherine's guard. What is your name and who is your master? You best answer truthfully if you wish to see your home and family again."

The young man took two steps back before speaking. "They call me John LeRune. I am a poor stable hand fetching water and hay for my master's horses. Renne, the stable master, lives in the village. He serves the queen."

Marcelle stared at John. The boy looked suitably frightened. "You seem a truthful lad. I seek two escaped prisoners, a man and a woman. The man is middle aged about thirty with light hair and complexion and the woman is very beautiful. She may appear royal to an untrained eye like yours. I am going to ask you nicely. Have you seen them, helped them find a horse, or heard where they intended to go? If you have, tell me everything you know and you may live."

We watched John tremble at the thought of what Marcelle might do to him. The boy remained silent, scrutinizing every inch of the guard who was much taller and much stronger. Marcelle's face proudly wore the scars of battle.

John cleared his throat. "I never seen no man or woman, only a band of three men. One wore in green, one gray, and the last in brown." He scratched his head. "They stopped at the inn. Sometimes ol' Matt lets beggars have bread and water. They gave me a penny to care for their horses. They went before sunset. I swear on my grandmother's grave, I am telling the truth. That's all I know. I swear on it."

Marcelle faced John whose wide brown eyes filled with tears from fear. "Umm, if I show you a map, can you identify the location?"

John shook his head. "I cannot read. I only know by signs, signals and distances. Show me the map, and I'll do my best to help."

Marcelle opened the small skin map and placed it back on the wooden worktable in the center of the stalls. He pointed to the 'X', the location he believed to be the head resister's cottage.

"There is a cottage here I must find."

John studied the map, moving his fingers from the drawing of the village square to a patch of drawn tall trees.

"Here's the village," John said. "We be to the side of the square. These trees be the forest. If the 'X' is where you want to go, you must head straight to the thickest part of the forest. Turn to the setting sun. When the brush thins, there's a path. You can see a cottage from a small hilltop."

Marcelle studied the young man's face. "I have dealt with many prisoners both innocent and guilty in my time. You seem honest."

The young stable hand sighed and appeared relieved as Marcelle flipped him a penny?

"You serve your queen well, boy. I am going to signal for my troop. They won't understand my methods and may hurt you thinking they can extract more information out of you. Go before I blow this whistle."

John took off like a shot. Marcelle put his high-pitched whistle to his lips and blew. The other guards, who were scattered, came running once they heard it.

When all were inside the barn, Marcelle discussed his plan of action. "All right, men. It appears luck is on our side. That traitorous blacksmith's cottage is not far from here. I discovered a hidden map. After studying it carefully, I feel sure we should enter the forest over there and continue until the woods become less thick. We will make a turn toward the west and continue until the cottage becomes visible from a small hill. We can ride most of the way there. When we get close, we dismount and surprise the traitors on foot at my cue. Does everyone understand? Are you ready to do our job for the queen?"

The other five guards nodded. "For Her Majesty Queen Katherine, and her powerful wizard, Alasdair," they shouted.

Marcelle led them out the stable door. "Let's find those traitors. If luck will have it, we may end up with the entire band of resistors as well."

I held my breath wondering if Marcelle would capture them all. Georgina and I watched as the six experienced guards mounted their horses and rode deep into the forest. They stopped by a stream to rest for a short while and refill their water flasks before heading to the point where they would turn. Once they arrived at the spot where the cottage came into view, they got off their horses tying their leads to nearby trees. The guards emptied their saddlebags of sharp knives, rope and water flasks, items they could carry in a small sack bound by a leather strap around their shoulders. Marcelle lined them up before holding his hand up to signal that they were to follow him.

# Chapter Thirteen

Georgina looked at me. "We now know what those men are up to and where they are going. That gives us the advantage. I shall ask the cards how close I can place you to Simon's cottage to avoid danger. Are you sure you're ready for this? You may not come home this time."

I took a deep breath. "Yes, more than you know. Aidan risked his life to save mine. I love him and must do the same for him"

Georgina stood, held me by the shoulders and looked directly into my eyes. "All right then. Listen to me very carefully. When I place you in the forest, you must walk a short distance west until you see Simon's cottage from the hill. Your position will be on the opposite side of the field from Marcelle and his men.

"Get as close to the cottage as possible. Look for Aidan. When you see him come out of either the house or the barn, try to get his attention. You need to draw him into the woods near you. Once you are together and have his undivided attention, tell him he is in danger and that Alasdair's men are on the other side of the field waiting for him.

"You must reveal right there and then that you are a Traveler who fell deeply in love with him and have come back to save him. Make sure he knows it was Alasdair who abducted you from another time to suit the queen's needs, and you have now returned with the help of a good friend and skilled sorceress. We both know I'm not a wizard, but this is the language he understands. Are you all right with this so far?"

I nodded as my body trembled from the mere mention of Alasdair's name. "Yes, please go on. I'm listening."

"Good. I have to give you the dreaded rules of Travel. You have never Traveled with me before so I must warn you. Once we start, there is no turning back. You may stay as long as you need to help Aidan escape from Alasdair's grasp, but you must tell Aidan time travel is the only way you can be together safely and share your love for the rest of your lives. He has to understand and be willing to Travel or I cannot make this happen. Understand?"

I gulped a very weak 'Yes' before explaining. "I did try to tell him when we first met but then never felt the urge to mention it again. Almost like Alasdair put a spell on me to forget."

Georgina nodded as if she knew. "A spell so that you wouldn't ask for help. This spell of his was to last just long enough to do the queen's bidding before he sent you into obscurity. However, when you held my card in your hand and called out my name, that spell was broken and no longer good. Once I help you and Aidan escape and Travel through time, I need that nasty man to follow you here to face me directly. I hope you both will help me break the spell of my body's confinement in wood and keep his spells away from all of us. Now enough talk about that evil man."

By this time, I was in tears, brought on by the memories of our attempted escape and that awful wizard. I wanted to be with Aidan but voiced my concerns to Georgina.

"But what about Aidan? How will he cope in our time? So much is different, so much will seem strange."

"Listen to me carefully, Danielle. Love has a way of getting through all of that. You did all right in his time. You adapted because you loved him. All that matters is that you love each other very much and wish to spend the rest of your lives together.

"Once you are in his time, after you signal him, take him someplace you can be alone—a field, a forest. Then call me. Remember, for me to come get you, you each must call out to me by name and tell me you are ready. "Georgina Ready." Got that?"

"Leave the rest to me. If you find you get into any kind of trouble earlier than expected, call my name for help as you did before. My psychic channels will be open. I will be alert and listening for you. Do not wait until the last second. I am a gypsy fortune-teller, not a magician, and things can go wrong.

"One more thing. When you speak to Aidan about leaving, you must ask him to tell me that he loves you and wants to spend the rest of his life with you. That's very important. Then hold hands and call out "Georgina Ready." Do you understand all this?"

I nodded my head. "Yes. Yes, I do and I am ready."

"Oh and I'd appreciate it if you didn't refer to me as the dummy like you do with the customers."

She had a way of making me laugh. I needed that now more than ever.

"You got it."

Georgina made a quick turn and bumped into my side. Her bump hurt so much I had to tell her.

"Ouch. Trying to kill me before I even get there?"

"Oops. Sorry, Danielle. Now let's get you to Aidan."

She smiled. I gave her a thumbs up.

"Good, now face me with your hands on your sides."

Georgina touched the seven cards that were fanned out on the counter. I watched those beautiful colored lights appear again and race around the walls. As the lights raced faster, she closed her eyes and chanted.

"Oh wonderful kind spirit in the cards, please come to us. Help Danielle find her true love. Take her back to Aidan. Take her back to his time. Help her bring him back to us here. Please come now. We need your help."

All I remember hearing was Aidan's name before I was whipped up in a cyclone of air. I whirled around over downtown Naples. My hometown looked like the miniature village we set up under the Christmas tree. In a matter of seconds, I floated into the clouds watching intently as different periods of history whizzed by me. Then... Thud.

Thud doesn't aptly describe what a crash landing does to your body. I landed rather awkwardly much like a pelican only on hard ground in the thickest part of the forest instead of the warm waters of Naples Bay. I thought of those clumsy birds and how they crash into the bay looking for fish. Lucky for them, water provides a much softer landing. I straightened myself before standing.

I had to act fast. I was back in Alasdair's timeline. I rubbed some dirt on my face hoping to make myself invisible.

My first task was direction. I had to find Simon's cottage. The forest can be very confusing. Aidan had taught me to be aware of sights like crooked tree limbs, sounds and smell. Suddenly a strong waft of lavender filled my nose.

Georgina did say west. That's it. Marie's wonderful garden. I followed my nose like a bloodhound tracking a scent until I reached the edge of the forest. From the brush, I spotted Simon's cottage.

I had to be careful of my approach. I hoped Aidan was there and I would see him come out of the cottage or barn alone. I waited patiently. It took some time. Every minute seemed like an eternity, but I knew I had to wait if I wanted to rescue the love of my life.

I remembered Georgina's warning. Alasdair's guards lay in wait for Aidan somewhere nearby. I remained hidden crouching down and staying as quiet as possible. I listened for the guards' trademark whistle and heavy footsteps. When I did not hear anything, I thought it safe to proceed.

If I wanted to save my lover's life, I had to risk mine. I felt confidant since I now had a secret weapon—Georgina. Cautious, I crawled through the field of tall brush in the direction of Simon's cottage, hoping for a glimpse of Aidan.

I lay low when I heard the crackling of leaves.

"What was that?"

Heavy footsteps approached in the dried brush. I hoped it might be an animal, but from the heaviness of the steps feared the worst. I remained close to the ground trying to hide from whoever was approaching. The rustling sounds indicated there were more than two people. I looked over at the path to count all six of the guards.

How could I handle six guards alone?

I soon heard gruff whispers.

Marcelle spoke. "I order you to stay on this side of the hill where we have a better view of any comings and goings. We will keep a watchful eye from a place a little farther from here. Always keep our mission in mind. Save the girl. Kill the traitor!"

The guards cheered. The more they cheered, the angrier I became.

Marcelle continued. "When I found that map, I knew we had them. Alasdair will be pleased we also found an important link to their underground. He wants that lying knight to be executed, but I'd like to kill him myself right now for all the trouble he has caused our beloved queen."

An even gruffer voice responded. "Better not. Better do as Alasdair instructed. We can all surprise that traitor and lock him down. If he resists, Alasdair said then, and only then, may we kill him. If there are other resistors at the cottage, they will not have our weapons or enough time to prepare for our surprise attack. We might be able to take them all. Once we have the knight, he will lead us to the princess. She can't be far away. They are lovers and cling to each other for strength. When we have them both, we'll head back to the castle."

Marcelle agreed responding, "Follow me."

I covered my mouth trying not to gasp. My love. If they reach him before I do, they will kill him. I'm sure any excuse they can muster for Alasdair will do. I had to get to Simon's and warn Aidan before they find him.

Once the guards' footsteps were out of earshot, I stood. I could see through the trees they took a wrong turn and went off course. I scrambled down a small hill toward Simon's as quietly as I could. I stopped every so many steps to listen for anyone who might be following me. I did this all the way to the clearing.

Once there, I ducked in the thick shrubs near the edge of the forest staring directly at Simon's cottage and the stable. I waited patiently until I saw Aidan come out of the barn. He looked well and as handsome as ever.

At first, I almost didn't recognize him. He looked relaxed and dressed like a peasant. Our absence made him more appealing to me than ever. I couldn't waste time staring at him. I had to warn him about Alasdair's guards and hoped he would trust me about Georgina. My pleading had to succeed so she could bring both of us home.

He walked closer to where I hid and began to dig up truffles. I crawled, moving forward in the brush to get closer to him.

He yelled back to Simon in the barn. "Hey, Simon, I have to get closer to the forest's edge to pick Marie some more of those delicious truffles. Don't worry, I'll be careful. No one even knows I'm here."

Aidan left the open field and approached the edge of the forest where I hid in the shrubs. I tried to whistle as best I could in the hopes of copying the sound of Simon's men, but my first attempt to get his attention failed. I refused to give up.

This plan had to work. I tried again. Aidan stopped short when he heard my second whistle. He looked around. He's smart enough to realize Alasdair's men wouldn't signal. They would just surprise him.

As he approached my location, he spoke quietly. "Who goes there? Speak. I know by your signal that you are an ally."

I watched his eyes comb the area trying to locate where the sound came from. When he came close to the where I hid, I tried it again. He stepped farther into the brush missing me by inches. That was my chance.

"Psst. Aidan, it's me. Danielle. I'm a fugitive just like you, but I have a plan for our escape. Please come to me. I did not desert you. I went for help so that we could escape together."

Aidan paused trying to locate where I was. "Where are you?"

"Over here. Look down." I raised my head.

"Are you part of a royal trap? There are many stories circulating about you in the village. I thought you left me for another man."

"Never. I would never do that. I love you with all my heart. Besides, why would I risk my life to come back for you? You are the love of my life so I guess you're stuck with me. Besides, if I were part of a trap, they'd have you by now."

I could see Aidan smile.

"Was this man and your escape with him just rumors to fuel town gossip?"

"Yes it was gossip made up to separate us. There was no man. My help came from a woman who intends to help both of us escape. I trust her with my life and yours. Now come over here you stubborn fool. Come here. I'm in the bushes."

Aidan was at first reluctant, but soon walked to me. I held my two hands out and grabbed his ankles pulling him down to the forest floor. I slid over and rolled on top of him planting the longest, most sensuous kiss of my life on his lips. To his surprise, I covered his mouth with my hand. I wanted to present the plan without interruption.

"You have no idea how happy I am to see you, but you must not speak until you listen to everything I have to say. Alasdair sent six guards to find you. They have orders to take me back to the queen and kill you if you resist imprisonment in any way. Luckily for us they took a wrong turn, but will return at any moment. You must believe this. Nod your head 'yes' if you do."

I gave him no choice. I gently shook his head up and down. When I let go, he laughed. I covered his mouth again.

"This is not a joke. I must tell you this before our lives are placed in jeopardy. Remember when I said I was from a different place? I was telling you the truth. You did not believe me, but Alasdair put a spell on me afterwards never to tell you again.

"You must listen to me now. I am from the New World, a place called Florida, but also from a different time. My time is 2015. That's hard to imagine, I know, but the queen is not the only one with a wizard. I too have an incredible sorceress who rescued me from Alasdair's grasp. She pulled me into the future and back to my time. When I told her my story, our story, I asked her to help us be together and she said she would do so. Do you understand this so far?"

Poor Aidan. I could see by the confused look in his eyes he thought I had lost it. I know he believed in wizards so my plea stood a good chance.

"Now please remain quiet. No arguing. We face grave danger. Alasdair's men are all around us and can find us at any time."

Aidan remained puzzled, but looked at me kindly with those gorgeous blue eyes pleading to uncover his mouth. I relented and took my hand away.

"I more than anyone am aware of how much danger we are in," he whispered. "You say you are from the future. I don't know about that. I love you so much I believe you have your wits about you or seem to. I believe in you. I do not know what to think about the future or wherever you came from."

"Looking back, however, you did arrive out of nowhere in very strange dress. I have trouble understanding you even though we both speak French. At first, I thought you came from a different country, a territory of France perhaps, but another time begins to make more sense. I've heard a skilled wizard can Travel through time. Now all those odd things you did and said are understandable. You say you have a sorceress, is that because you are a princess?"

"I do not like to think that way. She has become a trusted friend and I consider her an equal."

"How kind of you. Another place and in the future no less, tell me more about it. The wizard Alasdair has told us many wonderful tales about the future after he returns from Travel. The more I listened, the more I hoped to go."

I felt like I was getting through. "Good because now's your big chance. The best thing to come out of all of this is that we'll return together. Now, please stand up so we can leave here unnoticed. I'll tell you more at our first rest stop."

Aidan nodded and stood before helping me to rise. We walked as far as we could away from the cottage before stopping at a spring for water. I told Aidan more about my real life.

"Florida, my home, is a lovely warm place that is no longer under Spanish rule. It has beautiful white sand beaches and tropical flora. I am a merchant with my own shop selling articles from the past. Alasdair came to me under the pretense of selling a dagger when he kidnapped me and took me back to your time and Chenenceau. He knew of my royal lineage. My grandmother told me I came from royal blood but I never believed her."

Aidan's interest in my story piqued. "But you do not live as a princess now?"

"No. I live like a happy and busy commoner. I love the way I live. It gives me freedom to work as I please and fall in love with whomever I please. My wizard's name is Georgina. She's a gypsy seer who pretends she is made of wood to fool people while hiding her true powers. Her skills are as powerful as Alasdair's and she will work hard to keep us together."

"Here's what she said we needed to do. While we are free of Alasdair's men, we must hold hands and call out to Georgina by name for her to come for us. You must call out to her and tell her that you love me and want to spend the rest of your life with me."

Aidan looked pleased. "You know that's what I want. That's not hard to do. You are the love of my life."

I wanted to make sure he understood exactly what was involved. "Those words are easy to say, but remember we will be spending that life in the future in Florida. That's the only way she can make it work for us. You must tell her that or face the consequences of Alasdair's men."

Aidan took my hand. "Danielle, I do want to be with you more than anything. I risked my own life for that. 2015? What will I do for work? How will I fit in? Simon will think I was captured or abandoned him. Those thoughts are daunting."

"Georgina will help you with Simon."

Aidan nodded. "As long as Simon will know I'm all right. I will adjust to the rest. He did so much for us. I'm ready to go as long as we can go together."

He held out his hands ready to leave this chase behind.

I couldn't respond. Something startled me.

"What was that? We must hurry. I hear footsteps approaching from the woods. We must find a safe place a little farther away from here."

We started to run, but unfortunately, we were too late. As Aidan reached for my hands to call out to Georgina, the rustling noises caught up with us. I rolled into some tall brush, but Aidan did not follow. I watched in terror as Alasdair's men rushed him and held him to the ground. They bound his hands before helping him upright.

Marcelle pulled Aidan's head up by his hair to look at him. "Did I hear you had an accomplice, traitor? Shall we comb the bushes?"

Aidan wrestled to free himself but couldn't. "I am here alone. No accomplice. She left me for another man. Haven't you heard?"

I caught Aidan's glance. Terror filled his eyes. He looked back at me; his eyes pleaded for me to remain quiet. The guards milled around poking through every bush looking for me. I heard their noisy footsteps come close to where I was hiding. Then I heard hooves. The guards stopped. Someone of importance had arrived on horseback. Chills went up my spine when I heard a familiar voice. It was Alasdair.

"I know that royal wench is here somewhere. I can smell her frightened flesh. That smell keeps me going. Guards, keep looking. When she utters the slightest sound out of fear, we'll jump in and take her. I'm sure neither of them is armed."

127

I knew I could escape the wizard's grasp by calling Georgina, but I refused to leave Aidan behind. The wizard's horse stopped. He got down and walked near where I hid. I felt the air heat from his hot breath. He crushed the leaves with his bold strides and heavy black boots. As his footsteps neared, I covered my head with leaves for dear life. I was shaking.

When I looked up, Alasdair was standing right over me glaring down with those horrid red eyes. He stepped on my hand keeping his heavy foot there. I yelled in pain.

"Over here, men. Quick she's over here. Marcelle, take charge and get her."

His men scurried to reach me. They surrounded me commanding to stand. I refused, yelling and screaming. Two of them manhandled me, bruising my arms and legs as they picked me up. I kicked as hard as I could, but not hard enough for them to let me go.

"Grab her now, you imbeciles. Grab her by her hair. You two stay with her. Make sure her hands are bound."

Marcelle called for one of his men to take me from the other guards. After he did, he pulled my arms behind me and tied my wrists with rough rope. The rope burned my skin. I tried to wriggle free but couldn't.

Alasdair ordered the others to get the horses. I followed them with my eyes and spotted a royal carriage and driver on the hill. I froze as Marcelle pulled me toward the carriage with the other guard following. I heard Aidan yelling for them to stop.

I looked over at him. He was bleeding and lying on the ground not too far from the coach. I saw the look of frustration and anger in his eyes and hoped he would remain calm and not do anything rash that might get him killed. I winked when I walked by. He no longer resisted. He understood why he should stop.

I remembered I had a fountain pen in my pants pocket. I tried to work the rope enough to loosen the binding and regain the use of my hands. I was careful and, painful as it was, loosened the rope enough to free my hands. I didn't want to do anything unless I was sure I could overtake the two guards. Reaching in my pocket, I grabbed the pen.

What? Another card? That's why Georgina bumped into me.

Georgina worked like the gypsy pickpockets of Europe. Only, she put something in my pocket rather than take out anything. I touched her card for luck, but could not read it now. I had to use every ounce of strength and wits to get us out of here. I took a deep breath.

I never hurt anyone before, but it was them or me. Holding the pen like a knife, I thought I might have a chance since surprise was on my side.

Surprise worked. I stabbed Marcelle who was still holding the rope on my right side. He refused to let the rope go so I stabbed him again in his wrist. I must have hit an artery because blood came spewing out of the wound. When he held the cut with his other hand, he released the rope completely.

The other guard rushed forward, but I had already pulled the knife from Marcelle's belt before the guard came close enough to help. When he did, I stabbed him. Once both guards were disabled, I ran over to Aidan.

His guard turned when he heard the others yell for help, but I was on top of him before he could attack me. I stabbed the guard in his side with the knife. The guard doubled over in pain and let go of Aidan. Aidan got up, loosened his rope, and grabbed my arm. As we ran into the forest, we could hear the three guards yell for assistance.

"Help! We're bleeding. The prisoners have escaped. Come quick. Help us."

There was loud chatter before heavy footsteps ran through the leaves and into the forest after us. Alasdair's men pursued hot on our heels. We ran as fast as we could through the forest to a clearing before coming to a screeching halt at the edge of a tall cliff.

# Chapter Fourteen

We froze at the cliff's edge. We looked across the ravine, wondering if we could survive a jump. The gap was too wide. It looked impossible. Upon closer inspection, the ravine possessed the most beautiful waterfall hugging its other cliff and facing us. For a split second, the movements of the crystal clear waters mesmerized me with their beauty.

Aidan scoured the ground and trees near the cliff looking for anything that might help us. He separated a heavy vine from a group of vines attached to a nearby tree. He pulled on it with all his weight to see how strong it was before tying it around my waist and his. I looked at him hoping he wasn't thinking what I think he was thinking.

Aidan looked determined. "We have to jump. It is our only hope. This vine should be strong enough to carry us across. If not, the very worst case, my love is that we'll be together in another world rather than another time."

I panicked. Did he even look down? "Should be strong enough? How about will. I hate heights and the thought of drowning even more. I guess I forgot to tell you that when we were getting to know each other. I don't think I can do this!"

I changed my mind as soon as I heard the guards approach. We had no other option. I looked at the waterfall one more time. Its sprays created mini rainbows, their colors a kaleidoscope against the afternoon sky. Aidan took my hand. A funny feeling came over me. I took Georgina's card from my pocket. Son of a gun if she didn't hit the nail on its head one more time.

*Be Fearless. Believe in yourself. Believe in me. I'll protect you.*

*Georgina never lies."*

How does she do that?

I looked at Aidan and whispered, "When we jump, tell my sorceress Georgina that you believe in her powers and that you love me and want us to be together. She will protect us. Trust me."

I could feel Aidan's fear through his touch. His hands shook. I didn't know what terrified him more—the jump or 2015. Imagine leaving a time you know well to enter a universe you can't even imagine exists. When he spoke, I was amazed at his bravery.

"Now let's do this. Are you ready? Don't look down."

How could anyone in her right mind be ready for this let alone not look down? It had to be a one hundred foot drop.

Aidan continued. "On the count of three, grab onto me as tight as you can. We jump together. Ready. One. Two. Three."

Alasdair's men ran toward us. They were getting close enough to reach out and grab us. I threw my arms around Aidan's waist and held on as tight as I could. We took a running start and jumped.

I looked back at the guards who seemed to move in slow motion shooting arrows down at us. We were swinging across the ravine at a rapid pace. Our vine gave us enough support to let us swing far enough away from the cliff to prevent the guards from cutting it. We dropped down deep enough to avoid being hit by their arrows. Then what I feared most happened. The vine snapped by itself but did not break. We dropped down at a chilling pace clinging on by a thread.

I shouted in Aidan's ear. "Tell Georgina how you feel now. Right now. Tell her. She's listening."

"Georgina," Aidan nervously yelled out, "I believe in you. I love Danielle. I want to spend the rest of my life with her." He repeated it one more time.

Oh, how I hoped Georgina would not let us down. Our branch snapped once more making us drop deeper with every breath. Why didn't his call to her work? I remembered I had to call as well.

I looked up into the sky before closing my eyes and shouting, "Georgina I believe in you. I love Aidan and want us to be together forever."

By now, we were descending at the speed of a crashing airliner. The rocks in the riverbed were getting too close for comfort. I saw Alasdair watching from the top of the cliff. I thought I heard his evil laugh.

I called out to Georgina again shouting the words she needed to hear as loud as I could. The second I finished, a soft gust of wind came out of nowhere and positioned itself underneath us like a cloud. That soft wind came to save our lives. Georgina could not have cut our rescue any closer.

Soon another wind, a magnificent strong wind, blew past Alasdair and his guards knocking them to the ground until it reached us. I watched that cyclone of air approach before it swooped down, with all of its strength, picked us up, and lifted us skyward.

Aidan looked surprised but relieved. We clung to each other as we rose above the waterfall, and flew over Alasdair who was shaking his fist in anger.

"Georgina I heard them call out to you. I am not done with you yet."

That evil man heard my last plea for help.

We kept going up. Up over the top of the other side of the cliff from Alasdair's men. We sailed through a circle of colored light, a beautiful whole rainbow created by the mist. The rainbow colors of pure yellow, red, blue, and green became more vibrant as we rode the wind through them. The mist cooled my head.

Aidan kept a tight hold on me as we ascended to a small soft puffy cloud. That strong wind dropped us gently on the cloud. Its surface felt as soft as silk on my skin. We sighed, relieved to be away from the wizard as we flew above the tall forest trees and over the river. We ascended higher into the atmosphere, the air cool and comforting.

We soon flew over familiar places, Simon's, the village, and the castle all looking like miniatures from our bird's eye view. Cool breezes wafted through our hair while gentle mists refreshed our faces as we flew through multiple layers of soft clouds. All of a sudden, we stopped.

"Don't be afraid," I whispered to Aidan. "We must be almost there. We will experience a quick drop. It's all right. I've done this before."

We descended at a rapid pace. I saw downtown Naples. My heart was in my throat. I looked behind us hoping Alasdair was not following us. No one came into my view. So for now, I just wanted us to make it back to Georgina safely. Our special wind became noisy alerting us we were approaching homeport.

We spun around and around until—THUD!

We landed hard on the floor of my store right in front of Georgina's fortune telling machine. She stood over us as we lay on the floor, hands on her wooden hips.

"Well, it's about time you two arrived. What took you so long?"

I looked at Georgina in total disbelief. "What took us so long? You pull the strings. Remember?"

Georgina chuckled. "I saved you in the nick of time, didn't I? You both hesitated to say those magical words for such a long time."

She stopped talking and walked around Aidan, obviously curious to see what he was like. "So this is your Aidan. You have good taste Danielle. Handsome lad if I say so myself."

Georgina winked at him. He looked up at her uncertain how to respond.

"How are you dear? I'm Georgina. I placed thoughts of your safe escape to England in Simon's mind for you. He believes that is where you are."

She held out her hand to help him up. Sure. She'd help him up. Never mind me. I could stay on the floor forever as far as she's concerned.

Aidan took her hand, stood up and stared into her kind face. "Georgina is that what you call yourself? Thank you for that. Simon is a good friend. You are the most beautiful sorceress I have seen. You are a life-sized doll who wears no black nor covers her face in a veil. I'm delighted and honored to meet you, my lady." Aidan bowed.

"Likewise I'm sure." Georgina responded.

Aidan saw me still sitting on the floor and held a hand out to help me up. Once I stood, he hugged me as tight as he could before kissing me.

Georgina cleared her throat. "All right you two lovers, save that for later. We have serious work at hand. I'm quite sure Alasdair heard Danielle's last call to me and now realizes I was behind both rescues. He is most likely planning to follow you once he gets permission from the queen. You must remain by my side and continue to be brave to help me break our two spells. Remember, he cast a spell on me four hundred years ago, turning me into this wooden mannequin. By breaking my spell, I can then break the hold he has on the two of you and prevent him from coming here to bother any of us ever again."

I was apprehensive about what we might have to do, but I wanted to help Georgina and no longer desired to peer over my shoulder afraid of Alasdair's revenge. I looked at Aidan. He was engrossed in Georgina's words.

"Danielle, we must help this kind lady. Our lives will be spent in fear if we do not. I know it is a great deal to ask, but we must help the sorceress who saved our lives."

He reached for my hand. Georgina looked pleased.

"Please come over to the counter so we can plan our course of action. We have to work as a team, a unified team in order to break these outrageous spells. No one must deviate from our plan. Understand?"

Surfer scampered out of my office and snuggled between Aidan's legs. He picked her up and stroked her.

"Lady Georgina, I understand about magic powers. I have spent time with a powerful wizard, an evil one at that, and know how great and mighty these powers can be. I will do whatever you ask of me. Danielle?"

Aidan accepted Georgina's explanation easier than I did. He was accustomed to wizards and their magic. Even though I counted myself in, I was just a novice to all this.

"Georgina? Do you really have the powers to do all this?"

Georgina was miffed. "Of course I do. Do you think you would be back here safe and sound if I didn't? My powers can reverse his spells, but only if he comes to me of his own volition. He has to seek me out. That is the first requirement and that is where you both can help."

"I'm sure he heard Danielle's plea, and will follow to snatch her, take her back in time, and complete his procedure for the queen. However, he will face one big obstacle—me. I will be waiting for him eager to defeat him. At first, he will not be able to see me. I plan to hide behind the drape of my cabinet. Danielle, when the time is right, you must cover my cabinet in the same manner you did when you were angry with me."

Georgina smiled at that last thought.

"As a gypsy seer, once Alasdair arrives, I can perform the magic necessary to make me a whole woman again, while erasing you both, this store, and Naples Florida from Alasdair's memory."

Of course, I had to add my two cents. "That's like hypnosis by gypsy. Isn't it?"

Georgina kept talking ignoring my feeble attempt at humor. "To break my spell, I must take him by surprise and overpower him. My surprise will make him weak and temporarily powerless against me. Then, and only then, will his spell on me be broken. Once that's done, I can cast the spell that will save both of you from that evil man's wrath."

I was stunned. Everything she told me about her life was true. She had powers I couldn't explain. We watched her remove the lavender-colored crystal ball from her cabinet and place it on my counter. She closed her eyes waving her long fingers over it.

"Oh crystal ball. Show me through your magnificent powers where that evil Alasdair is right now. Show me now."

Wham! The crystal ball shot out rainbow colored rays of light like lasers circulating the room. Aidan and I watched with awe as the lights came to a sudden stop, rotated, and flowed back into the crystal ball. When the last ray of light fell back into the ball, the ball lit up as if it was about to explode. Georgina leaned in to take a look.

"Ahh. There he is. He's with the queen. Let me hear what he's saying. There, look close. That nasty queen is pointing her finger at Alasdair. She is demanding that he find you. His position in her court depends on his success. Good thing she doesn't realize she is only helping our cause by ordering him to come to us. Poor Alasdair is quiet. It's quite nice to see him that way for a change. He's probably unable to speak after that royal threat. He is telling the queen that he would be willing to search for another match if necessary. Look at that."

What? What is she looking at? There's room for only one person to look into her crystal ball.

"Danielle, the queen just stomped her foot and gave him a scroll with a royal decree. He has to obey. Alasdair bowed and said he would find you no matter how difficult the chase. He revealed to the queen that he believes he knows where you are and will journey into the future tomorrow to catch you off guard. Won't he be surprised when we set our lovely trap for him?"

Georgina watched the crystal ball go dark. She picked it up carefully, placing it back on the stand in the front of her cabinet. She turned to face us.

"Are you both ready to do this? Our task is not without risk. You understand this is your only hope of staying together without living in constant fear."

I looked into Aidan's eyes. He placed my hand in his.

"Yes," we both said

"Good. That's very good. Now, Danielle, I'll need that drape to cover the cabinet and some blackboard chalk. Aidan, do you have anything Alasdair gave you personally when you were in the queen's guard?"

Aidan at first shook his head negative, but then his eyes lit up. "Yes, I forgot about this."

He removed something from under his shirt.

"Here, I have a charm on this chain I wear on my uniform belt every day. Alasdair gave it to me when I joined the guard. It is a serpent like the one on his ring. The charm designates which guards work for both the queen and her wizard. He said it has the power to locate me whenever needed. That's probably how he found our ship. To be honest, I forgot about this since it has always been attached to my belt and I could only afford one leather belt. At any rate, Alasdair said never to take it off. He will always be with those who carry his insignia. He said the charm would bring me luck and save my life. I guess it works since I'm here and not facing the executioner."

Georgina cracked a smile from ear to ear. "We want to keep you here, but how fortunate for us that he will always be with you. Tell me, did that nasty sorcerer touch it?"

"Why yes," Aidan answered her truthfully. "He rubbed it and put a spell on it before presenting the charm to me."

"May I have it to use in our spell? Please give it to me. I promise to return it when we are finished."

Aidan looked at the charm. "No need to return it, my lady. It's of no use to me now. I want nothing to do with that man."

Aidan took the charm off his chain and handed it to Georgina. She put it on the stand next to her crystal ball.

"Thank you. Now go refresh yourselves and change your clothes. Aidan will find suitable clothing on your bed, Danielle. Please, both of you get some rest. You will need every ounce of strength to get through this."

I wasn't thinking about danger right now, just my rumbling stomach. I was starving.

"I'm hungry and need something to eat."

Georgina scowled. "I can't eat so I am sure there is no food here. If you walk out that door to buy some, you will be placing yourself in danger because you will be out of range for my protective powers."

I looked around. She was right. There was nothing to eat here except food for Surfer. That didn't matter to Georgina. She was wood. I was hungry. I needed food.

"Suppose I order take out and have you pay the delivery man with money from the cash register."

"What will that messenger think when he sees a wooden mannequin handing him money? What if the delivery man was sent by Alasdair to trick us? Maybe that man is Alasdair in disguise. I can think of all kinds of harmful scenarios. Besides, if I get the weakest feeling your delivery man is dangerous, I'll destroy him.

"You know I can't pay the delivery man and you call me a dummy. If he's someone you know, tell him to knock, leave the delivery on the front step, and pick up his money from the box near the front door. Tell him you are ill and cannot come to the door."

"What do you like on your pizza?" I asked Aidan.

Aidan looked at me as if I was speaking Chinese to him. For a few minutes, I had forgotten about our time differences.

"Never mind. I'll improvise"

I walked over to the phone on my counter and dialed a familiar number. "Hey, Sam. It's Danielle. I know I haven't called in a while. Been on a trip to France of all places. Say, I'd like to order a large extra cheese pizza, thick crust with three bottles of water and a large mixed salad. I'll need paper plates and plastic ware for three. I came back with a nasty cold so the shop is closed. Have Ted knock three times so I know it's not a customer and leave the box on the front step. There'll be money in my mailbox in an envelope for him. Are you all right with that? Great. Thirty minutes? Perfect."

I looked at Georgina. "I ordered enough for the three of us just in case. I'll take money from my change bank and put it in my mailbox with enough for Ted's tip as well."

Georgina looked sad. "I appreciate your thought, but I cannot eat. I have not needed nor been able to enjoy real food since Alasdair turned me to wood. After tomorrow, that will all be different. You'll have to order enough for four."

I went to the register and put a note in for the cash. I placed the money in an envelope and wrote Ted's name on the front of it. I opened the front door a crack and slipped the envelope inside the mailbox. I grabbed Aidan and left to shower and change in my office.

I saw Aidan peek in my small bathroom with no tub and step in the shower.

"Where do the buckets of water go? I'll carry them in."

I smiled. "Water comes out of that funny looking pole. Look I'll show you."

I turned the shower on. He jumped back.

"That's magic. From Georgina?"

"No. The water company. Everyone in my time has this. Now come here and let me scrub your back."

He did and we showered together lathering each other with lavender soap and shampoo. We kissed before dressing. I made up the sleep couch just in time.

The pizza delivery showed up exactly thirty minutes after my call. Ted knocked on the front door three times. I waited until I thought it safe to retrieve the pizza box. Aidan and I ate as if we had never seen food before. He said the bread, cheese, and tomato were delicious. Poor Georgina had to watch. I'll make it up to her if we survive our next crisis. She advised us to get some sleep. She requires no sleep, so she will have everything in place ready for Alasdair's visit.

# Chapter Fourteen

When I was a prisoner in the castle, just the thought of Alasdair bursting into my room unannounced made it difficult for me to sleep. However, Aidan and I had been through so much, we were exhausted and fell asleep as soon as our heads hit our pillows at six that evening.

A few hours later, there was a persistent knock on my office door. We woke up. I sat up and looked around. It was still dark.

"Hurry," Georgina called through the door. "Get dressed. It is eleven fifteen. We have to be ready before midnight. Alasdair is a tricky one. He loves the element of surprise. I wouldn't put it past him to arrive at one minute past midnight our time."

Aidan and I shook the cobwebs from our minds and dressed before making our way to see Georgina. She was alert, organized, and as sharp as ever. She stood next to my counter in the dark. The only light we saw came from three large candles of different heights and colors. Georgina lined them up in a straight row next to each other. She motioned for us to approach her.

My knight reached for my hand. "I believe with all my heart this amazing sorceress will bring an end to our trials."

I gazed into his wonderful eyes. "I'm sure you're right. I've come to trust her with all my heart as well."

Georgina motioned again for us to come and stand close to her before explaining what she expected us to do. "I need both of you to stand to the right behind my box and the line I drew in chalk on the floor. Until I break the wizard's spell, my powers can only protect you from Alasdair as long as you stand on that spot and only that spot. Do you both understand the seriousness of my request?" We nodded.

She pointed to the candles. "These three candles on the counter each have a special meaning. The pink one symbolizes my freedom from Alasdair's spell, the white one is for the freedom and longevity of your love, while the black one is for Alasdair to be banished from here and from history, taking his vain queen with him, never to return, never to remember who we are and what we do. As their flames die, the unlit candle signifies my spell has taken hold. We will not be safe and cannot take any chances until all the flames have been extinguished. Please respect that."

We listened and nodded mesmerized by the flames and the soft monotone sound of her voice as she spoke.

"I looked into my crystal ball a short time ago and saw he had already left the castle. I am sure that at any minute, he will be here with us. I am frightened yet exhilarated at the same time. I have dreamed of this moment for over four hundred years."

I looked out the front windows of the store. The streetlights flickered before going off. Georgina raised her hands when they flashed on again.

"Now hurry, he's here. Cover me and the machine with the canvas. Take your places. Hurry as if your lives depended on it because they do. He is very near. I can hear the sound of his bats' wings."

At first, I didn't hear anything, but it took mere seconds for me to hear the fluttering of wings as they approached our location. Georgina stood tall behind her cabinet while I covered her with the drape.

She spoke softly: "Both of you close your eyes and believe in my spells. Believe they will happen. Believe in my powers. That will make them stronger."

We did as she asked. We stood firm behind the chalk line with our eyes closed, mine so tight they hurt.

By now, the fluttering noise deafened us. I was scared out of my mind and clung to Aidan when the front door blew open and then slammed shut by an evil wind. Loud heavy footsteps approached. The same ominous footsteps I had heard many times before. They entered and approached the counter.

When the footsteps stopped, I opened my eyes. Aidan did the same. I could feel his body tremble. He was as afraid as I was. We have both seen first-hand what this evil wizard was capable of doing.

Alasdair grinned as he approached us.

"Who goes there? Is that Alasdair? The notorious master wizard of evil?"

Surprised, he stopped when he heard Georgina's voice come from the back of her machine. Alasdair looked around scouring the immediate area to see where she was hiding. His eyes turned red with anger, but he stood still staring at us. I knew Georgina wanted him to approach her so she could put her spell on him, but she diverted his attention from us by making her voice come from the front of the store.

"I repeat. Who goes there?" she asked sternly.

Alasdair turned to look around again. I could tell he was cautious.

"Why is that my beautiful Georgina? You may try to surprise me, but your voice is one I can never forget. You refused me as a lover, remember? Now you are wood. How different your life would have been as my partner."

Alasdair walked over to her cabinet and bent over to see what was under the drape. "I can see your cabinet. It is dark, but I know you are stuck inside. I am surprised by your fluent speech. Did you tire of 'Georgina Never Lies'? Did another cast off part of your spell? I am sure they cannot remove the entire spell so I am still in charge. Tell me, what is it like to never feel love, emotion, or human interaction? I will give you another chance to be my bride. After all, I am a forgiving man. Say yes or I will have to get rid of you and the knight before I whisk Danielle back to the castle in one efficient spell."

Alasdair rubbed his hands together as he approached us. "My beautiful Georgina, those two traitors are standing in front of me next to your cabinet. I am going to remove that drape. I deeply desire to look into those beautiful glass eyes of yours one more time and admire my masterful work before I kill you and the knight and take Danielle. Tell me Georgina, do you wish to be alive as my bride or disintegrated into wood chips?"

Alasdair stepped closer. Too close for me. I could feel his hot breath. I knew as he approached me that he approached Georgina as well. That's exactly what she wanted. He did not know she had the power to come out of her machine. That was her secret.

He grabbed one side of the drape and pulled it off quickly. Taken by complete surprise, he jolted back when he did not see her inside. He turned, stunned to see Georgina walk out from behind her cabinet. She stared into his eyes as she lifted her arms toward the ceiling.

She spoke with authority: "Beautiful Ceresin, my purest spirit, show Alasdair your strength and your powers. Cast a spell on him to make him helpless. Weaken his powers, diminish his strength."

Georgina pointed her hands toward the ceiling, moving them back down toward Alasdair. He was frozen, surprised to see her step out of the cabinet. Lightning bolts crashed down from the sky through the ceiling and passed through her hands before entering the wizard's body. Shaking, he fell to the ground. Georgina stepped out into the candlelight. She looked as beautiful as ever, but she was angry.

"Look at you lying helpless on the floor. You are a poor excuse for a wizard. You'll soon be a little man. You will have no powers in here or anywhere…not in this time or anytime. I will make sure of that. You may have tricked me four hundred years ago even though you were aware that my powers were greater than yours. I have now proved that to be the case.

"When Danielle called out for my help, she was the charm that released secret powers I placed in myself when you turned me to wood. Those powers helped me leave my wooden box and activate other powers I used to save her from you. These powers have always remained my best-kept secret. I am sure you of all wizards remember the force of dueling spells. Now that you have come to me, I have the power to nullify you, your queen, and your selfish spells. Danielle was the bait I used to hook you."

Alasdair remained on the floor still shaking from the lightning bolts unable to move or speak. Georgina touched her crystal ball, releasing multi-colored lights that swirled around the room at a feverish pace. She waved her hand over the wizard. Alasdair's body froze where he lay. He tried to wave his arms, attempting to hide his eyes from the magical lights that negated his powers, but couldn't. Georgina approached him.

Standing over him, she stared into his red eyes. "Alasdair, I have turned the tables. You will have to deal with me now. As I look deep into your eyes, you will begin to feel drowsy. Your body will become weaker. Your powers will become as weak as your body. You will not fight these feelings. As you drift off into a trance, you will understand the power I have over you. You will through your subconscious remove forever the spell you cast upon me not just for this moment, but forever accepting the fact that my powers are indeed stronger than yours. You will, when the lights stop, break the spell you placed on me never to cast it again."

Georgina waved her long arms over the sorcerer. She touched the crystal ball. The swirling lights came to an abrupt halt before going dark. I looked over at the candles on the counter. The flame on the pink candle extinguished at the same time. I looked over at Georgina.

She waved her hand over herself. An intense streak of bright light clouded my vision. When my vision cleared, Georgina was a flesh and blood woman, a beautiful regal one. Now dressed in a royal blue gown, she put her head down for a moment before standing tall, walking to the front door, and stepping outside. I knew she wanted to test her newfound freedom. She returned in an instant determined to keep the wizard under control.

Looking at Alasdair still lying on the ground, motionless, she shouted, "I went outside for a breath of fresh air. You can no longer stop me. I can breathe, my skin feels soft, and I feel wonderful. I am whole again. I have broken your spell. Now, my powerless wizard, tell me again what you plan to do to my lovebirds."

Alasdair appeared as if he had been drugged. He tried to speak but could not say any words. I glanced over at the two remaining candles. The white and black candles were still burning bright. I watched Georgina having fun and feeling strong as she walked around Alasdair poking him with an antique walking stick I kept near the counter. She wanted to make sure he remained weak and powerless.

She leaned in and spoke into his ear. "How does it feel to be as still as wood?"

Feeling safe, she knelt down and touched his head with Aidan's charm. "Alasdair, when you feel me touch you with this charm, you will go into a deep trance. You will erase Danielle, Aidan, and this store from your memory as well as the queen's. You will forget about Danielle's shop, Naples, Florida, and what you and Queen Katherine of

143

Chenenceau intended to do to Danielle. As far as you know, Sir Aidan never was born.

"As I wave this charm over your head, you will never again want to come to this time and place. You will lose all desire to chase them. As I hold my hand over your head, I will make this lapse in memory carry to your queen. The deeper the trance, the more you both will forget. History will forget about the two of you. You will be sent to a parallel universe where you will have no power. Let your mind go deep, deep…deep. Aidan and Danielle no longer exist in yours or the queen's mind."

She waved her hands around again and whispered some words in a language I couldn't understand. I looked over at the white candle. The flame flickered and died.

Georgina breathed a deep sigh before putting her head down on the counter.

When she raised it, she looked at Aidan and me. "You are both safe. Your love is secure. I am drained but I must continue."

The only candle left burning now was the thick black one. She stretched her long slender fingers before speaking.

"Alasdair, the remaining black candle is in your honor. I know you can hear me though you are unable to speak. A fitting spell, don't you think? After all, Georgina never lies."

"I hereby banish you from this time, this place and these people. You are never to return. You and your selfish queen will be banished from any history of the castle living in your own time warp. You will, however, remember me but only out of fear. You will never want to see or meet me again. My powers frighten you."

Georgina reached down and touched the wizard's head with her hand. "Do you understand? Nod your head if you do."

I watched in silence. I could see Alasdair's eyes were closed. Though the rest of his body was immobile, he nodded his head. His body remained as stiff as a board. I looked over at the black candle just as its flame flickered and went out.

Georgina took a deep breath. "Alasdair, when I snap my fingers, you will come out of your trance. Fear will overtake you. One look at me and you will tremble as you call for that evil wind and your bats to take you back to your time warp."

Georgina laughed. "Ready you old ugly goat?" She snapped her fingers.

Alasdair opened his eyes. I didn't know what to expect. Fear overcame him. Sitting on the floor, he moved away from her as fast as he could. He whistled for that evil wind with every crawl. Suddenly, my front door burst open. We heard his black cyclone approaching along with the fluttering of bat wings. The bats stared at us as they entered the store, but refused to fly too close. The cyclone blew into the store.

Vases crashed and small furniture smashed against the walls. Throughout this mystical chaos, Georgina stood tall bracing herself against the cyclone. Aidan and I ducked down behind the counter to get away from its wrath, but she faced the evil wind head on—her long black hair blowing in its gusts.

The wind swirled until it stopped directly over Alasdair. Its winds moved with such speed that we could no longer see the wizard. The black cyclone picked him up and thrust him into its wicked wind. I watched his attack bats fall into formation around him. Up they went before flying out the front door as if sucked out by a vacuum. On their way, the power of the cyclone destroyed statues, tore apart books, and broke china.

Aidan and I had to hold onto whatever was near us for dear life. When the last gust blew out the front door, we all breathed a sigh of relief.

Georgina spoke first. "This spell should have exhausted me, but I am invigorated by all our good news. You both are safe and will remain so. I owe you both a debt of gratitude for helping me remove Alasdair's evil spell. You cannot imagine how wonderful it is to feel alive and whole again. I can never repay you."

Aidan looked into my eyes as he spoke to Georgina. "You already have, my dear lady. My eyes are filled with tears, tears of joy. Thank you for giving me the love of my life. I hope to make Danielle my wife."

I stared into Aidan's eyes. "I love you Aidan with all my heart. You are my lover, my best friend, my hero. I will be honored to be your wife."

I've always been such a private person, I can't believe I said all that in front of Georgina but she knew it was true. Georgina looked at both of us with kindness.

"Aidan and Danielle, your love is earnest and pure. It will last all of your lives."

She held up her hands. As she did, I felt a warm wind pass through me. I could tell Aidan felt the same thing. He smiled as the wind left us.

Georgina continued. "Your love has now passed the test of the winds of time. You will have a long and happy marriage. Danielle, I will make sure I restore your store to the way it was before Alasdair's visit."

She closed her eyes. We did the same. Soft winds circled us as we heard strange noises. When I opened my eyes, the store looked back to normal.

Georgina looked at us. "I can now leave knowing you both will fare well."

I could not let that happen. "Georgina, I'm shocked to hear you say that. I've come to love and trust you as a friend. I don't care about being used as bait, only your friendship. Besides, who will be my maid of honor? Where will you go?"

Georgina thought for a few minutes. "I do not want to go back to my time. There is nothing left there for me. I probably will wander through time looking for somewhere suitable to stay."

"Stay here with us. Take my apartment in the back of the store. Please I cannot bear the thought of losing you, of never seeing you again."

Georgina looked pensive. "What will I do here? I am not meant for this time."

"Yes you are. You can help me here in the store reading the fortunes of my customers just as you did in the gypsy camp. Maybe you'll help some other lovers like us find true happiness. Maybe you will find your own soul mate."

Aidan moved close to Georgina and kissed her cheek. "Besides you have to be at our wedding. You are the reason we can celebrate."

Georgina took both our hands. "I seem to be the happiest when I am with you both. Our adventure is a bond we will never break. I promise to stay here as long as I am useful." Georgina laughed. "I have a funny feeling in my stomach. It's making noises I haven't heard for a very long time. Oh my, I must be hungry!"

I laughed walking over to the cash register for some money. "You should be. You haven't eaten for four hundred years. There's a twenty-four-hour diner one block from here that serves enormous portions. Let's go."

I took Georgina's arm. The three of us walked out the front door feeling free and exhilarated to be rid of Alasdair and his magic once and for all.

# About the Author

Ever dream of traveling through time? Mariah Lynne does. She writes stories that take her readers along on exciting journeys. Travel to distant times and beautiful places with strong-willed independent heroines whose memorable tales will entertain with twisted plots that dabble in the paranormal. *Shadows Across Time* fits that description to a T as do her previous works *The Love Gypsy* and *The Duchess' Necklace*.

A Graduate of Syracuse University, Mariah lives on a beautiful Florida Gulf Coast Island where she has written weekly entertainment columns for two island newspapers. Because she loves where she lives, Southwest Florida takes center stage in her stories.

She is a member of Romance Writers of America and the Southwest Florida Romance Writers who recently published an anthology: "*From Florida With Love*: *Sunsets and Happy Endings.*" Mariah's short story "Love At First Flight" is included.

When she is not writing, she enjoys swimming, traveling and spending time with her husband and her dolphin hunting dog, Max. To learn more about Mariah and her Time Travel adventures visit her at:

Website: www.MariahLynne.com
Twitter:@mariahlynne1
E-mail:MariahLynneAuthor@yahoo.com
https://www.facebook.com/pages/MariahLynne/295721153858612